CHARWE

By

Elton Ndudzo

First published in Great Britain in 2024 by:

Carnelian Heart Publishing Ltd
Suite A
82 James Carter Road
Mildenhall
Suffolk
IP28 7DE
UK
www.carnelianheartpublishing.co.uk

Copyright © Elton Ndudzo 2024

Paperback ISBN   978-1-914287-83-1
eBook ISBN   978-1-914287-84-8

The right of Elton Ndudzo to be identified as the author of this work has been asserted by him in accordance with the Copyright, Design and Patents Act 1988.

A catalogue record for this book is available from the British Library.

All rights reserved. No part of this publication may be reproduced, stored in a retrieval system or transmitted in any form or by any means, electronic, mechanical, photocopying, recording or otherwise without prior written permission from the publisher.

Editors: Memory Chirere and Samantha Rumbidzai Vazhure

Cover art: 'Great Zimbabwe Ruins 2' (2024), by Samantha Rumbidzai Vazhure
Cover layout: Mike Stuart

Typeset by Carnelian Heart Publishing Ltd
Layout and formatting by DanTs Media

To the Canadian Crew: Ashley, Tadiwa, Moila, Audrey and Nothabo–

Hold on to all your dreams. The sky is the limit.

Contents

The Gathering Storm	9
The Dream	16
The Hwata Court	23
The Maneless White	33
When Destiny Calls	39
A Roar From The Past	45
The Initiation Ceremony	51
The Pool named Peace	62
Mukwerera	70
The god of the Sun and the Moon	77
The Farewell	82
The City of Kings and Queens	86
The Thrashing	93
Fort Martin	99
The Fall of KoBulawayo	104
The Sting	109
The Coronation	114

The war council	121
The Attack	126
The Hand of Justice	131
The Falling Bones	137
The war of Murenga	143
The Union Jack	155
An Oath of Return	163
The Trial	167
The last supper	173
The Execution	179
Afterword	189
Acknowledgements	190
About the author	191

THOSE WHO APPEAR IN THIS ACCOUNT

CHARWE NYAKASIKANA, a woman of the Hwata Dynasty
CHIRI, her brother
KEMU, her brother, heir to the Hwata Chieftainship
MUTIMUMWE, other brother
HUNGWARIRI, her firstborn son
TANDI, her second son
SVOTWA, her last-born girl
MASVI, a former police officer
MAZARURA GOREDEMA GWINDI, her chief
MEDA, an advisor at the chief's court
TAKU, a madman
CHINENGUNDU MASHAYAMOMBE, a Zezuru chief
GUMBORESHUMBA, his spiritualist
MATOPE, another Zezuru chief
HENRY HAWKINS POLLARD, a native commissioner
BLAKISTON, a police officer
FATHER RICHERTZ, a catholic priest
LOBENGULA KHUMALO, king of Mthwakazi
LOZIKEYI DLODLO, his chief-wife
MLILO, His right hand advisor
MUKWATI, his court advisor and spiritualist
KAPFUMO, the Hwata royal spiritualist
SELOUS, a police officer
WATERMAYOR, a judge at the court of Salisbury
HERBERT HAYTON CASTENS ESQUIRE, a public prosecutor

1

The Gathering Storm

"A war is coming!" The man shouted as he ran through the village, his body covered in ash and rags, waving his hands. Most of the villagers merely exchanged glances, shrugs, and muttered dismissals.

"Poor Taku," one woman who had been winnowing her grain sighed, shaking her head.

"Another bout." They all had grown accustomed to his madness, and so they continued their daily activities, unfazed. Little children made fun of him and followed after him, their feet kicking up dust as they mimicked him, "A war is coming! A war is coming!"

But Charwe felt a cold shiver running down her spine after hearing the man's cries.

Charwe was well aware of Taku's madness, but his words reminded her of her strange and haunting dreams. Blood-

soaked fields, screams swallowed by smoke, a monstrous shadow engulfing everything…
—A war is coming!

The madman's shouts cut through Charwe's thoughts. She took a deep breath, trying to calm her pacing heart. Charwe looked up at Chiri who was walking next to her, seemingly unfazed just like everyone else. *That is because he doesn't know*, she told herself.

Charwe turned to look at the setting sun in the distance, wondering if she should just tell him. The sun painted the sky in varying shades of orange and red. It was a beautiful sight, though she noticed little, for her mind was somewhere else.

She always shared all her secrets with him. Maybe he would understand, maybe he would help her make sense of them.

Chiri was her brother, as both their fathers, Guba and Chitaura had been brothers, sons of Shayachimwe Mukombani, the great conqueror.

Charwe still had her gaze on the distant horizon. Chiri strode by her side, his hands clasped behind his back, calm and composed as he had always been.

Chiri must have noticed that something was troubling Charwe and he was quick to ask her. "Is there anything wrong? You don't look at ease."

Charwe shook her head and forced a smile. "Nothing's wrong, Chiri. I'm just tired. It's been a long day." He nodded, but she could tell he wasn't convinced. Chiri was quite a clever man and knew her too well to be fooled by her lies.

Charwe could easily see the concern in Chiri's eyes. She knew how much he really cared for her. She wanted to tell him about her dreams, but was afraid of what he might say, or worse, what he might do afterwards.

"What are dreams?" she found herself asking, as they walked past some women who were grinding grain in large drum-sized pestles.

Chiri's eyes suddenly sparkled with curiosity, and a gentle smile formed on his lips. "Dreams are like intricate tapestries woven by our minds as we sleep. They are stories that emerge from the depths of our memories, our emotions, and our deepest desires."

The ground shook to the pounding of the pestles, and it was in rhythm with the songs that these women sang.

"There are dreams that are said to transcend mere stories," Charwe said. "How can one possibly know that they have such dreams?"

"That is a question for the experts, like Kapfumo," Chiri told her. "I only know that those dreams are very important and must never be ignored."

Charwe was not a spiritualist like Kapfumo, and she tried convincing herself that her dreams were just stories. She tried to convince herself, yet, deep within, she harboured an unwavering belief that there was something more to them.

Chiri looked at Charwe with a gentle expression. "So tell me, when did you start having troubling dreams?"

Charwe's heart lurched. "I, uh... I don't dream," she stammered, her voice cracking.

Chiri just gave her a simple smile, very much aware that she was not being honest. He decided not to question her further because he could clearly see that it made her uncomfortable.

He knew that she was going to eventually tell him about her dreams, another time. He knew her very well.

"I haven't seen you at court in quite a while," Chiri said, starting a new topic.

"Why torment myself with those droning sessions?"

"Meda would be there," Chiri said, a glint of mischief in his eyes.

Charwe's eyes flickered momentarily. "What? Why would I care about Meda being there. He is the least interesting person at court."

"Is he?" Chiri asked, his mischief smile still on him.

"Tell me about Kemu," Charwe said. "How's the heir of our great dynasty doing?"

Chiri sighed. "Not well, it seems. His duties overwhelm him. And Chief Gwindi's temper, as you well know, isn't exactly soothing."

Charwe shuddered. "I can't imagine. Always under scrutiny, always performing. I wouldn't trade my freedom for that gilded cage." She turned to Chiri, her eyes earnest. "You're always by his side, aren't you? My brave, strong brother."

"I can't shield him forever, Charwe. He needs to learn to stand tall on his own. Poor Kemu, he's as timid as a field mouse. He can't even pretend to be strong," Chiri sighed, a hint of sadness in his voice. "I always tell him, the world only sees the mask you wear, not the face beneath. The Chief is hard on that boy because he lacks confidence."

"Perhaps Kemu understands that we shouldn't wear a mask that doesn't fit our face," Charwe offered. "We shouldn't pretend to be something we're not. A blade is a blade, and a leaf is a leaf. You might be good at pretending, but there are those like us who aren't really good."

"But you must all understand that the world preys on the weak," Chiri countered. "Perhaps a predator might hesitate to attack a bushbuck wearing a lion mask, whether it fits or not. If you want to survive in this world, you have to be strong. And sometimes, the only way to be strong is to pretend."

"The world is what it is, harsh and cruel," Charwe gave a sigh.

Before she could continue, a sharp scream came from the end of the village

"What was that!" Chiri said, as he moved to stand directly in front of Charwe.

Within the blink of an eye, the whole village erupted in chaos. Everyone was screaming and running. Chiri looked up in the distance and saw a group of armed warriors running towards the village.

"The Ndebele raiders!" Chiri cried, when he noticed the long shields and spears that the men held. The raiders had been running into their village, attacking and capturing any man they saw. The Ndebele raiders had been from a military kingdom to the south of their land, Mthwakazi. It was the strongest in the territory. Chiri took Charwe's hand, then ducked with her behind a nearby rock, trying to stay out of sight.

"Stay here," Chiri said, his face fierce. "I've got to go there and help the others."

"You can't?" Charwe held his arm. "You've no weapon,"

"Well, I have to do something," Chiri said. "I can't just hide here. I have to protect those people." He started to stand up, but Charwe pulled his arm. "No," she said. "There are too many. They will capture you and take you hostage, like the others."

Chiri really wanted to do something, but he knew that Charwe was right. The best thing he could do was to hide and wait for the raid to end, or he would end up being dragged to Mthwakazi as a hostage.

"I guess you are right," Chiri said, then huddled together with Charwe behind the rock, listening to the sounds of raid.

Chiri felt bad, just hiding there, and hearing the villagers crying, women screaming as their husbands and boys were taken away by the raiders. He could hear the crackling of the thatched huts burning and the bellowing of the cows that had been taken from their kraals.

Charwe closed her eyes and covered her ears. The smell of smoke was thick in the air, as the sun slowly hid itself beyond the horizon. It was all just as she had seen in her dreams. The smoke. The screams. The shouts.

At last, when she opened her eyes, the sun had already set, the screams had turned to wails, and the raiders were gone. Her whole body shook, as Chiri lifted her from where she had huddled herself.

The raiders had taken as many men and livestock as they could. Chiri held Charwe's hand, as they walked throughout the village, looking at all the damage. It now had been dark, but the fire of the burning huts made everything visible. The village was in ruins.

"These raids have been intense recently," Chiri said, seemingly confused. "Something is not right. Why are they even taking the men?"

"A storm is coming," Charwe said, looking at the smoke rising in the night sky. "That's what the man in my dreams said to me. A storm is coming."

Chiri stopped and looked at Charwe. "Tell me more about your dreams."

Charwe shook her head. She didn't want her dreams to be of any consequence. "There is nothing, just fire, smoke, darkness and men without knees."

"Men without knees?" Chiri could not understand.

"Every night," Charwe said, with tears threatening to spill from her eyes. "I see them coming out of a vast body of water, like none I have seen before. They are followed by a swarm of locusts and meerkats digging holes everywhere. I see stars falling like burning embers and igniting everything. I hear the voice of the man in the wind. A storm is coming, he always says."

"Have you told anyone about these dreams?" he asked her.

"No, I haven't," she said, then a tear dropped from her left eye. "I wanted to tell Kapfumo, but I always feared that he would tell me that they meant something. They shouldn't, they are just death and destruction." Chiri then hugged his sister, knowing that it was what she needed at the moment. He told her not to worry, even though he himself was now worried.

A storm is coming! She said.

A war is coming! The madman shouted.

He knew it couldn't just be a coincidence.

2

The Dream

Charwe reached her village, and the thoughts of the raid she had witnessed still haunted her. She hugged herself tightly, feeling the cold bite on her skin.

She walked past some huts, and she could see the faint glow of fires inside some of them, but most were now dark and silent.

She finally reached her hut, then pushed her wooden door and quickly stepped inside, away from the cold. It was pitch black, except for a sliver of moonlight that came through her small window. She then smiled when she looked down at her three children, who were all fast asleep.

She took a pile of dry grass and twigs by the doorway and placed them into the fireplace in the middle of the hut. She struck a flint against a stone and lit a fire. The flames cast a warm flickering light inside the hut.

She looked at the face of her young strong boy, Hungwariri. He was overprotective of his younger siblings. He was so young and innocent, and she never wished for anything bad to happen to him.

She thought about what she had seen, and about the mad man's screams, as well as her dreams. She knew that something big was coming, and she didn't want it to take her children away.

Charwe removed the covering from a clay pot by the fire and saw the meat that they had left her.

Svotwa was a good cook, and Charwe always liked her food, but that day, she didn't have an appetite. She covered the food and pushed the clay pot away with her leg.

Charwe was never going to have an appetite for food until she was well assured that Hungwariri, Svotwa and Tandi were all safe and away from any troubles.

She sat down by the fireplace for a little while as she warmed herself, thinking about everything.

She then laid down on her mat next to her three children and felt the rough texture of the straw against her skin. She wanted to sleep so that she could stop thinking about the screams that she had heard. She sang a song to her children, even though they were all asleep. It was a song about an old baboon with eight children, climbing up mountains and looking for food.

The story really never had any sense, but it helped to calm herself, and after a while, she was able to drift into her own dreams.

Just like the previous night, she found herself enveloped by a thick mist. There were large boulders of stones around her, and they seemed to be balanced, one sitting on top of the other.

She looked around, trying to make sense of this place, trying to find something. She then saw an eagle sitting on a tree branch nearby. The bird had black and white feathers, and a red face and beak. The mist made it hard for her to see, but she noticed that the bird stared at her with piercing eyes, as if it knew something she didn't. She was afraid, but she found herself taking a step towards the bird.

But before she could get any closer, the eagle spread its wings and flew away, then disappeared into the mist.

She then saw men marching past her. She could not see their hands or their faces, for they had been covered with the mist. She could only see their legs, but she couldn't see the knees on them. The men disappeared in the mist, and then she heard distant screams and wails.

"The end is coming with a storm," she heard a deep voice from afar. "The storm is near and looming larger. It's bigger than any storm that has ever passed through our lands. This storm is here to stay."

The voice seemed to come from everywhere, and nowhere. "A storm is coming," the voice kept saying. At first it came from her left, then from her right, then from behind her.

"Who are you? Show yourself. What do you want with me?" Charwe shouted, looking all around her, wanting to see something, anything.

"What I am matters not, only what you are," the voice said, then it moved closer to her ear that she could almost feel its breeze. "Woman, do you have any conception of the power you hold, of the great destiny that awaits you? You are the maneless white."

She turned around again, hoping to see someone. There was nothing, just the mist, and the balancing rocks.

"Stop tormenting me, leave my dreams and never return. Please stop this, I beg of you."

The voice then came again. "You and I are woven from the same strings; we are of the same nature. I'm reaching out to you just as you are also reaching out to me."

Charwe was frightened, then closed her eyes, wanting to escape from that place, wanting to be back in her hut, on her mat. She managed to pull herself from the dream, then found herself opening her eyes, and it was morning.

Charwe stood up from her sleeping mat, her dream still vivid in her mind. She stretched her limbs and yawned, then got up. Her children were still sleeping, except for Hungwariri, who had already gone to get the firewood. Charwe decided not to wake them up, and walked to the door, as she tried dismissing the thoughts of her dream.

She opened the door and stepped outside, feeling the sun's rays caressing her skin, which was darker than mahogany. She leaned against the door of her hut and looked around, the thoughts of her dream still tickling on the surface of her skin. She saw the other villagers busy pounding their grain, weaving baskets and making pottery.

A group of women walked past her in a single file with water vessels balanced on their heads.

"Mangwanani!" Each of the women greeted Charwe with smiles as they walked past her.

"Mangwanani!" Charwe smiled back at them warmly. As soon as they walked past her, her smile quickly died out, as her dream had been overshadowing all her thoughts.

Mangwanani, that was the usual and ancient question everyone used to greet one another in the morning.

The question was an old Zezuru dialect, meaning "who has the words?"

The question was very important in the days, when many of the people received important words given to them by their ancestors through dreams. The people would share their dreams after being asked, *"mangwa anani?"*

If one had not received any strange dream, that person would throw back the question, *"mangwa anani?"*

Charwe had thrown back the question to the women, yet she had the words. To her, it was very clear that her dream was not just a dream but had been a message from some spirit. She shook her head and tried to dismiss these thoughts. She then noticed Hungwariri coming towards her from a distance, with a bunch of firewood over his shoulder.

"*Maita*, Samanyanga!" Charwe called out, a warm smile spreading across her face. She went on to take the firewood off his shoulder. "My elephant, the great beast. The one who shakes the world with his feet, who uproots trees with anger. Thank you, my son."

Hungwariri smiled, as he always loved it when she praised him with poetry, even for something as little as finding firewood.

One day, he vowed to himself. *One day she will sing my totem praise song after I do something bigger than this.* She carried the firewood as they both walked back inside the house. They found Tandi awake, already eating his mother's meat.

"*Mangwanani*, mother," Tandi greeted Charwe, his mouth stuffed with food. "You didn't finish your food yesterday, and I was feeling so hungry."

Charwe just shook her head, as she placed the firewood behind the door. "*Mangwanani*, Tandi." Svotwa had still been snoring from her sleep.

"I had almost forgotten," Hungwariri said, as he sat down on a bench to rest himself. "I met up with Chiri on my way here. He said you have to attend today's court session. He said that it's an emergency meeting, and all the Hwata family members should be in attendance."

"Oh," Charwe said. "It should be about the raid that took place yesterday. I should be getting ready then."

"I also wish to come," Hungwariri told his mother. "I'm old enough to be present at court."

Charwe hesitated, her gaze flickering towards the door. "Actually," she began, her voice low and hesitant. "I've been thinking. This place—it's not safe. Not anymore. You will all go and stay with my sister, your older mother, Chenge, back at her village. It will be for a little while."

Hungwariri's brow furrowed, and he rose to his feet. "What!" he exclaimed, his voice laced with disbelief. "Are you asking us to leave you? Svotwa and Tandi can go, but I'm not. Tell me, who's going to fetch water or firewood for you when we are gone? No, I'm not abandoning you like father did."

Charwe reached out, placing a gentle hand on his shoulder. Her touch was warm, yet a tremor ran through it. "Hungwa, please," she pleaded, her voice taking on a new firmness. "I have a bad feeling about the Hwata territory, about what might happen in the days to come. It's for your own safety, you and your siblings, believe me."

Hungwariri shook his head, his jaw clenched tight. Leaving his mother alone was unthinkable. He ripped his shoulder free from her grasp, his anger simmering. "I understand fear, Mother," he spat, his voice thick with emotion, "but I won't run, not from my mother. I won't run, I'm a different Samanyanga." With a final glare, he stormed out of the hut, slamming the heavy door behind him.

Charwe closed her eyes to the booming sound of the door, then turned, and saw that Svotwa had already been up, confusion in her eyes. Her voice was soft and trembling. "We are not going anywhere, right?" Charwe closed her eyes again and took a deep breath.

3

The Hwata Court

Charwe hurried to the court, hoping she was not too late. She knew the temper of her older father, who was her own father's elder brother, Chief Gwindi, and never wanted to provoke him.

Lucky enough, when she arrived at court, the Chief had not yet arrived. She was greeted by the usual sight of all the other Hwata brothers, royal advisors and elders who had been seated on their benches in a circle.

Chiri had been seated next to their eldest brother, Kemuteku. Kemu was the heir to their dynasty, and his face was stern, but his nervousness was clearly visible. Charwe remembered Chiri telling her that he was not good at pretending, and she could easily see that it was true. He clearly did not want to be there at court. He was a bit shorter than Chiri, but had a much darker tone to his skin, and had more curly hair.

Charwe tried hiding her own sadness, as she greeted her other brothers and court officials with nods and whispers. She tried not to think about what had transpired earlier, with her children.

The court had a golden thatched roof, and elephant tusks decorated its walls. On a raised platform, surrounded by the circular benches, the Chief's ivory throne stood in its glory. The air was filled with the fragrance of flowers that lined the walls.

Charwe's gaze inadvertently met Meda's, and her heart skipped a beat. She quickly looked away, feeling a twinge of annoyance. She hated how he had this effect on her, how she could never seem to control her reaction.

There was something in his eyes that made her feel both drawn and unsettled. She always looked away from them whenever they would meet her own. It was as if he could see right through her.

He seldom talked, even at court, and that made him all the more intimidating. He was a mystery she always longed to unravel, wondering what it was that lingered in that mind of his.

A horn was blown outside, and everyone rose to their feet.

Mazarura Goredema Gwindi, their Chief, entered the great hall with confidence and authority. He was tall and had an imposing figure, dressed in a beaded robe and leopard skin headdress. All the attendants bowed their heads and took their seats after the Chief took his own seat. Only Kapfumo, the royal spiritualist and advisor remained on his feet.

"Thank you all for coming on such short notice," Kapfumo acknowledged them all. He paused for a moment, allowing his words to sink in. Then he continued. "We've found it necessary to hold this emergency session, for our great Hwata dynasty is on the brink of destruction. We've been plagued by the drought, the locust invasion and rinderpest that is killing our cattle. To add to these misfortunes, the amaNdebele warriors are raiding our villages. We must find a way to respond to their latest attack."

"This impunity must no longer continue," one of the Hwata brothers, Mutimumwe, stood from his own seat. "The response is simple here, my Chief. We attack! We've men and arrows too, and we can fight. We just storm their capital and then we fight them and take back our cattle and men."

"We can't do that, Mutimumwe," Chief Hwata Gwindi replied. "I don't have to always remind you that Mthwakazi is a military kingdom, and we are its vassals. We can never rebel against it. They have complex war tactics that will bring the end to the remaining few men that we have."

Charwe was there, but the words exchanged just bounced off her head. Charwe's gaze shifted to the tapestries of wild beasts lining the walls, and then, she thought about her dreams. The blood-soaked fields, and the screams. Her fingers tightened around the rough fabric that covered her body, her breaths coming in shallow gasps.

Charwe wanted to stand up, and to scream at them, to tell them that she knew a real big war was coming.

She wanted to scream, but what right did she have to speak? Women at court were only allowed to watch and observe, and not to speak, unless they were asked to.

"That's why we need more fighters," Mutimumwe pierced through Charwe's troubled mind with his booming words. "We must merge alliances with other Zezuru Chiefs, attack the kingdom and obliterate it. We've been paying tribute to them for quite some time and now I say enough is enough."

"You are suggesting that we form alliances with other Zezuru Chiefs?" Chief Gwindi looked right at Mutimumwe. "Can you name any Chief out there who you think will accept that? Most of them are stubborn and the rest are cowards."

Charwe had been thinking about her son, and his stubbornness. If war would surely come, he would want to be on the frontline. Charwe knew her son too well. He thought he was a brave hero.

She wondered if he'd survive a battle. That thought turned her bowels, and she clutched the edge of her seat, trying to keep herself together.

It was then that Chiri stood up from his bench. "I suggest another route, my Chief. We are a dynasty because we are descendants of a conqueror. You can march against other chiefs and take them down just like our grandsire Shayachimwe did to Mbare and Zumbo. Once we take other territories, we will have enough power to strike Mthwakazi."

No, that would be wrong, Charwe shook her head.

They were all suggesting ways to start bloodshed to stop the raids. That wouldn't work.
Charwe's fingers traced the intricate patterns on her beaded necklace. Charwe didn't want to talk, but she felt a great urge. She tried biting her tongue, but she couldn't keep quiet, not with everything troubling her mind.

"War begets war, a truth we all know," she found herself speaking. "It will all be a vicious circle of people dying until we are all gone." A tense silence descended upon the room, and all eyes were on Charwe. Even the other women at court exchanged glances.

Charwe's heart pounded within her, thinking that Chief Gwindi was going to ask her to leave the court, but he went on to agree with her point. "At least someone at this court has reason. You are all suggesting we destabilise the whole region at a time we can't even afford a war. We have to find other ways that won't overwhelm us in the future. We must find the reason for these raids. One way to kill a tree is to cut its roots."

Chiri turned to Charwe, held her hand firmly and gave her a warm smile. What she had done was quite brave.

"Is it not obvious?" Mutimumwe responded. "We control the Shawasha gold fields and have established good trading relations with the Portuguese and now we have the Europeans. They want our power. They want to conquer us."

"Perhaps this is not about conquest," Chiri said. "If they wanted to destroy us, I think they'd have done that a long time ago. For all I know, they've never attempted to kill any Zezuru Chief, they are only taking the men and livestock."

"Haven't you heard about Chief Gomora, dear Chiri?" Mutimumwe asked, now visibly angry. "Or maybe you should be reminded of what killed him."

"Chief Gomora refused to pay his tribute, a duty that all vassals must all abide to," Chiri replied with quite a calmness. "He failed his duty, and the Ndebele merely enforced the consequences. It's obvious that their intent is to increase their military, that's the reason they are only abducting males of fighting age."

"And what would be the reason for them to increase their military if not to attack us?" Mutimumwe asked as he glared at him, his chest heaving.

"The amaNdebele have greater war skills than us, they would not need large numbers to take us down," Chiri said, then pursed his lips ever so slightly. "They can only increase their military if it's against an enemy that isn't us, a far greater and powerful enemy."

"Of course," Chief Gwindi realised. "The Ndebele now have sour relations with the Europeans after they executed Gomora. The Chief had been under the protection of the Europeans. They are the only power that Mtwakazi might fear, there is no denying that."

Charwe realised that Meda had disappeared from where he had been seated. She tried looking around the court, but he was nowhere to be found. He had sneaked out of the court without any of them noticing. *Where was he up to?* she wondered.

"Well, if they are not in good relations with the Europeans then it's good for us," Mutimumwe's voice took her from her thoughts. "We ally ourselves with the Europeans and take down the Mtwakazi kingdom once and for all. We should've already asked to be under their protection like the other chiefs. They have better firearms."

His words sparked a flicker of anger in Chief Hwata's eyes. "At what cost, Mutimumwe? Trade one master for another? The Europeans might protect us from the raids, but who will protect us from them? What reason should we trust them? They might not be our enemies, but that does not make them our friends."

"Then what?" Mutimumwe asked, looking right at the Chief. "Should we just sit on our hands while the Ndebele do whatever they like?"

"I was thinking that perhaps we could find common ground with the Ndebele," Chiri said. "My Chief, as you've said, one way to kill a tree is to cut its roots. Maybe you should send envoys to engage in dialogue and know the reason behind these raids. That's the best way to end this without bloodshed."

A heavy silence descended, thick enough to cut with a knife. Mutimumwe's fists clenched, his jaw set in a stubborn defiance. Chiri's calm demeanour held firm, but a flicker of worry danced in his eyes.

Finally, Chief Hwata spoke. "Envoys? No. I will go myself. Treat the Ndebele king directly." Mutimumwe's face remained stormy, but Chiri offered a hesitant nod, respect battling with apprehension in his eyes.

With a final murmur of agreement, the council dissolved, leaving behind the lingering tension.

As the room emptied, Chiri could still feel the phantom sting of Mutimumwe's anger and could only just ignore it. That had always been Mutimumwe's nature, disagreeing on things.

"Today's session was quite tense," Charwe said, as she walked with Chiri out of the court into the open sunlight. Her gaze instinctively searched for Meda. She found him a few paces away, laughing and talking with a woman. Charwe's heart tightened. That woman was probably the reason why he sneaked out of court. She couldn't quite understand why the sight of Meda with someone else stirred such irritation in her.

"You spoke in court for the first time," Chiri took her from her thoughts. "You are much braver than I thought you were, Charwe Nyakasikana."

Charwe glanced at Chiri and offered a smile. Yet beneath it, Chiri saw a flicker of sadness.

"Tell me, what's wrong," Chiri looked down at Charwe. "What's been bothering you?"

Charwe hesitated. Perhaps it was her dreams, perhaps her children, perhaps it was this woman that was making Meda smile.

"I'm sending my children away to my sister," Charwe said. "Only Svotwa and Tandi. Hungwariri insisted on staying behind, as stubborn as he always is."

"What do you mean you are sending them away?" Chiri couldn't understand. "I thought you'd always wanted them here, where they are safe."

Chiri saw that Charwe was not listening, and that her attention was drawn back to Meda and the woman. Chiri followed her gaze and chuckled. "Oh, don't worry much about that. That's just his sister."

Charwe turned to Chiri, her eyes sharp. "Why would I care who she is to him?"

Chiri's gaze softened as he studied her. "Do you think I do not notice the way you look at him? You have feelings for him, don't you?"

Charwe's eyes widened in shock. "What? That's absurd," she stammered, her gaze dropping to the scars on her wrists. "I once gave my heart to someone who nearly destroyed it. I won't make that mistake again."

"Not all men are the same," Chiri said gently. "Eventually, we all need someone by our side. Someone to love."

"I have my children," Charwe replied firmly. "They are the only ones I will always care for."

"And yet you are sending them away," Chiri pointed out. "Why?"

"It's for their very good," Charwe said, though her words trailed off as her gaze remained fixed on something. "Who is that?"

Chiri followed her line of sight and saw Meda with the woman. "I told you, that's just his sister."

"No, not her. The man walking with Zindoga behind them," Charwe said, her voice tense.

Chiri took a closer look and finally noticed the man Charwe had mentioned.

"Oh, you mean Mr. Pollard? That is a European if you've never seen one before," Chiri explained to Charwe "He is a friend of our Chief."

"Those legs, Chiri," Charwe said, her gaze still on this man. "Those are the legs that I see in my dreams. The legs of the kneeless men."

Chiri turned to Charwe. "What? Those dreams you told me about?"

"Yes," Charwe told him, now visibly shaking. "And last night I had that dream again. It's just the same, just that same old voice. The man that speaks to me never shows himself when I ask."

"When are you going to tell Kapfumo?" he asked, his voice filled with concern.

"I can't, I'm afraid," Charwe replied, her eyes filled with uncertainty. She was really scared.

"Of what?" he inquired, leaning in closer.

"Of what he'll say," Charwe confessed, her voice tinged with apprehension. "What if he tells me that I'm a medium? What if he insists that I must undergo initiation and spend my life performing rituals and interpreting omens? I don't want that kind of life."

He reached out and gently placed a hand on her shoulder, offering reassurance. "It's not always mediums who have dreams that transcend stories. Don't be afraid of anything, Charwe." With a slight hesitation, he handed her a small box. "This is snuff. Tonight, when you go to sleep, just take a little bit. It might help you gain clarity."

Charwe's eyes widened, and she instinctively tried to deny the small box. "No, I won't use snuff. It's meant for spiritualists."

He looked at her intently, his gaze unwavering. "Snuff is used to amplify your spiritual contact. If you use it, you'll discover whether your dreams are mere stories or something more profound. It's up to you, Charwe. Only if you truly desire to know."

Charwe pondered his words, her mind filled with curiosity and a hint of fear. Taking a deep breath, she reached out and accepted the box, her fingers trembling slightly.

She then turned again to the man with pale skin, and only one thing rose to her skin.
A storm is coming.

4

The Maneless White

Charwe was back in her hut, on her sleeping mat, warming herself near the fire.

She could hear the crickets outside, chirping incessantly in the dark. They sounded like a chorus of voices, reminding her that it was night again and that her dreams were coming again.

She was now all alone in her small hut. Hungwariri had escorted his siblings to her sister's place. It would be days before he would return. It had only been a day, and she already missed them all.

She looked at the fireplace, where a few embers were still glowing. She then reached out for the small box that Chiri had given her and looked at it.

He had told her that it would help her understand, but now she found herself wondering if she really wanted to understand.

She wasn't sure, but she found herself opening the box and taking a pinch of the brown powder. She hated the smell of it, but she had no other choice. She sniffed it gently through her nose, just as she had watched Kapfumo doing during his rituals.

She had been expecting something pleasant but then felt a sharp pain in her nose and a bitter taste in her mouth. She gasped and coughed, feeling dizzy and nauseous. She then sneezed violently, sending snuff flying everywhere. She felt her eyes watering and her nose running. She threw the box away in disgust and wiped her nose with the back of her hand.

The snuff was awful. Chiri had forgotten to tell her that part.

She then closed her eyes and tried to calm her mind. That night, she quickly drifted into her dream and found herself surrounded by that usual mist. She was standing right where she had been standing the previous night.

"A storm is coming," the deep voice came again without delay. "The hour of the prophecy is at hand, and you must take up your spear axe and prepare for the storm ahead."

This time, Charwe did not shout out loud, but spoke gently. "Who are you? Show yourself and end this mystery once and for all. I want to see your face, if you have it. I demand an answer."

As soon as she finished her words, she saw a man emerging from the mist in front of her. She gasped.

"I am your father, Murenga Pfumojena Sororenzou, son of Mambiri and grandson of Tovera the Great," he said as he walked towards her with the confident stride of a warrior. He had spiral white markings on his chest, which contrasted with his skin that was as dark as coal.

He looked familiar, but she couldn't really place him. She never knew Murenga, but she knew for a fact that he wasn't her father, as he had been telling her.

Charwe started walking backwards, shaking her head. "No, my father is Chitaura, son of Shayachimwe Mukombani. You are not him. You are not my father."

"Lift up your spear axe and prepare, for we are about to depart for war," the man said, as he slowly approached her. "Bees sting, and they sting for sure."

Charwe Nyakasikana was sure that she was probably speaking with the spirit of a dead man, someone who was trying to make contact with his own daughter.

"I'm sorry but I think you are lost. I'm Charwe Nyakasikana, a villager of the eland Hwata dynasty," she told him as she shook her head. "I'm not your daughter."

"You are who you are supposed to be, and where you are supposed to be," the man said. "You are Nehanda, the maneless white. Your roars are an ancient song, and it echoes throughout the whole land."

Charwe could see that the spirit of this deceased man was clearly confused. She closed her eyes and managed to drift herself from the dream as she had done the previous night.

She woke up with a start, her heart pounding in her chest. She looked up at the familiar patterns of her thatched roof above her and she smiled.

She jumped out of her bed, not caring about anything else. She had to inform Kapfumo about her dream.

The snuff had been quite horrible, but at least Chiri was right about one thing; it had helped her to understand. She was not going to be a spirit medium, no spirit of her ancestors wished to communicate through her.

She was only being tormented with a confused spirit. She quickly got up from her mat and wrapped her cloth around her. She prepared herself and hurried off to visit Kapfumo

Bursting into the hut without announcing her presence, Charwe found Kapfumo sitting on his mat, deep in meditation.

"You seem as if something has been chasing you," Kapfumo looked up at her, his eyes sharp and discerning. "What is it, dear Charwe?" She knelt before him, bowing her head, her breath coming in ragged gasps and her heart pounding like a drum.

"I'm sorry, Kapfumo. I didn't mean to disturb you, but I have to tell you something important." He nodded and gestured for her to speak.

"I need your help, Kapfumo," Charwe said. "There's a lost spirit that thinks that I'm its daughter, it comes in my dreams speaking about a storm and how I must prepare for it. You must help redirect the spirit where it really wants to go, to its real daughter."

The hut was dark and smoky, with herbs and bones hanging from the ceiling. There was a fire in the corner, where a pot was boiling.

"Charwe calm down," Kapfumo told her. "Explain plainly what you are talking about. I can't understand anything." Charwe then took a few breaths and started explaining herself.

"For all this time, I've been having strange dreams. I'd hear the voice of a strange man trying to talk with me, speaking in riddles and words I couldn't understand. I'd been afraid of them, because I thought that they might make me a spirit medium. But yesterday, the man came again and said that he was my father, who he clearly was not," Charwe laughed. "The spirit itself is confused because it thinks that it's talking to its daughter."

"I must admit my confusion," Kapfumo said. "This is my first time hearing such an issue. An ancestral spirit can never be said to be lost. It always communicates with the person that it intends to communicate with."

"But this spirit is clearly lost," she told him. "He is not my father because he is not Chitaura. He said that his name was Murenga Sororenzou, who clearly isn't even of Hwata origin."

"What did you say his name was again?" Kapfumo moved his head closer to Charwe, his expression now serious, almost worried.

Charwe felt a pang of doubt in her chest as she could see that his face had changed. Her voice trembled when she repeated that name. "Murenga Sororenzou."

"Child, do you even know the person you are talking about?" He asked her. "He is the most powerful spirit, the first leader of the Zezuru. He is the father of the Mhondoro, the maneless white lions that are guardian spirits of this very land."

Charwe shook her head, very much afraid, trying to deny the fact that was already clearly in front of her. "That does not imply that he is my father, does it."

"If he claims to be your father, then it means you are one of the maneless whites, you are a mhondoro spirit," Kapfumo explained it plainly to her.

Charwe felt a cold shiver run down her spine. "No, I'm Charwe Nyakasikana, a daughter of the eland Hwata dynasty," she denied. "I cannot be a maneless white lion. I'm just a normal villager! You've known me all my life, and this can't be possible."

"You will not just be a spirit medium, but one of the most powerful spirits to ever walk in centuries." Charwe opened her mouth to protest, but no words came out. She didn't know what to say anymore.

"Chief Gwindi must be informed right away. You are a mhondoro and only one of them is a female," Kapfumo told her. "You are Nehanda, the grandmother of all." Charwe shook her head in denial. She didn't want to believe it.

She didn't want to admit it, yet deep inside, she could feel it was true.

5

When Destiny Calls

Chiri and Kemu sat on a wooden bench in the courtroom, waiting for their older father, Chief Goredema Gwindi.

Kemu, as usual, was nervous and restless. He kept fidgeting with his cloth, adjusting his sandals, and glancing at the entrance of the Court. On the other hand, Chiri leaned back on the bench, looking calm and relaxed.

He looked at his brother with the corner of his eye and noticed how uneasy he had been. "It's not like you are the one who's going to the Ndebele capital. You should learn to control yourself and keep calm?"

"Our older father always comes late but expects me to be on time," Kemu complained to his brother. "I really hate being here at court."

"You should be the last person complaining about that," Chiri reminded Kemu. "Soon enough, Chief Gwindi will ride off to the south, and you'll be here, handling your subjects' disputes. Perhaps he might not return, perhaps you'll be the Chief of the Hwata indefinitely."

"Please stop talking about that. He will return," Kemu said. "And besides, you will always be by my side from the day I become Chief. I will make you my right hand advisor, and you'll always be here, helping me."

"No way," Chiri shook his head. "You will find other advisors to help you. I will be out there, in the wild, on an adventure."

Kemu laughed at his brother. "No, adventures in the wild are dangerous. You won't survive any day out there. A lion will feast on you, and won't leave out anything."

"Have you forgotten that between you and me, I'm the one who knows how to use a spear," Chiri said. "In the wild, I'd be in less danger than you are here. You might end up in a war with another clan, or continue on with our grandfather's conquest. I've heard that a Chief should lead his clan during a war."

"When I become Chief, the only spear that I would be required to use is the one between my legs. I only need to sire children," he replied.

"A lot of rulers died because of that spear," they both heard the deep voice of the Chief, as he walked into the courtroom. "That is every man's weakness."

They quickly got up and took a bow before their older father. Kemuteku squeezed his eyes with frustration. He had not intended for his father to hear those words. Chiri knew that Kemu was going to get in trouble for his choice of words, and the thought of that amused him.

Their older father nodded curtly and motioned for them to follow him to the front of the court, closer to his ivory throne.

"It was only a joke, my Chief," Kemuteku said to his Chief, Gwindi, as he took his own seat close to him.

"And with jokes, a lot of kingdoms crumbled to dust," Chief Gwindi said, as he sat on his throne. "To be a good ruler, you must be careful with your words, young man. These are dangerous times. Prophecies of war have never been this many. I hope we make peace with these raiders, for we do not wish to be in open war with them."

"Prophecies of war?" Chiri looked concerned, as Kapfumo, the spiritual advisor, walked into the courtroom.

The Chief's attention was drawn to Kapfumo, who took a bow before talking. "Your Highness, I come with great news. I've confirmed this morning that your niece, Charwe, is the medium of the great spirit of Nehanda."

Chief Gwindi's eyes widened. "Nehanda? The mhondoro spirit? Are you certain?"

"Yes, Your Highness. I have just sought confirmation from other mediums, and it seems to be true," Kapfumo said. "The guardian spirit of the people has returned, and we must initiate Charwe as soon as we can."

Chiri could not believe it. Charwe's dreams were not just stories after all. She was going to be a spirit medium, and by the looks of it, she seemed quite important.

"This is a very important matter," the Chief said, as he stood up from his seat. "We should inform all the Chiefs and clans about this. They must know that the great Nehanda spirit has chosen to be with us, the Hwata dynasty. They must come and pledge obeisance to my niece, their guardian spirit."

"This will be done immediately, your highness," Kapfumo said. "Charwe herself does not want to be a medium. The young woman is terrified. She demanded that I call Chiri for her. She said that her brother would understand her more than you, her older father and Chief."

"She probably will take time to understand what she'll become," the Chief said and turned to Chiri. "You shall go to her now. Make her see reason. Make her understand that this must be done."

"No, I can't," Chiri shook his hand. "I don't even know anything about this Nehanda spirit that you are talking about. Is it even of the Hwata ancestral lineage?"

"You can, and you will," Chief Hwata commanded. "You are the one who is very close to her and she'll understand you more. She has to know that it is not harmful to accept the destiny that her ancestors have handed her. It will not only be for her own good, but for the good of the whole dynasty."

"Is it truly harmless?" Chiri asked his Chief, concerned about his sister "What does this spirit do?"

"Great things," Gwindi gave Chiri a pat on the shoulder. "For now, just go to her, and make her see reason." The Chief then walked away with Kapfumo discussing their plans, leaving the two brothers together.

"Am I the only one who is unaware of what this hype is all about?" Kemu asked his brother. "What is this Nehanda spirit? It's certainly different from the other ancestral spirits that we are familiar with."

"I've absolutely no idea," Chiri replied with a sigh. "Yet I've to make Charwe see reason."

So, as he had been commanded by his Chief, Chiri went off to Charwe's homestead so that he would make her see reason. He found her in her hut, folding her arms against her chest, shaking. When she saw him, she quickly ran to him and threw herself in his arms, sobbing. She had been waiting for him all along. She really needed his comfort, and he had been the only person that was always there for her, in all her troubles.

"I've heard from Kapfumo," Chiri said, as he patted her back under his arms. He was very much afraid for her, and not sure of how he was ever going to make her see reason on something he himself never knew about.

"He doesn't want to understand," she told Chiri. "He has already sent a word to the Chief, and he plans on initiating me through a ceremony tomorrow."

"But why are you so terrified of it?" Chiri asked, trying to calm Charwe down. "It's just a ceremony, and being a spiritualist isn't all bad. You shouldn't be afraid, and everything will be alright."

"No, nothing can be right. Brother, I'm not the woman or spirit that he says I am, and I don't even want to be her. Something must be wrong with the dream, with everything. There has got to be someone else, someone who is fit to be Nehanda, someone not me."

"Do you think Kapfumo wanted to be a spiritualist? Do you think that our older father wanted to be a Chief? What about the young boys that are all sent to war, do you think they like it?" Chiri said. "Each and every one of us has a role to play, and we don't get to choose our own destiny."

"Please try to understand, or at the least, make everyone else understand. I don't want to become a stranger to you, to my children," she told him. "If you all fail to understand, I will run off to a faraway land where you won't find me."

"What are you talking about? Is Kapfumo a stranger to us?" He asked her. "Yes, you can run away, and maybe we will never find you, but your dreams will. They will follow you wherever you go, because they are you. You can't separate yourself from what you are destined to become."

"You've been the only person who's always understood me. Why can't you understand me now?" Charwe asked. "You know I've never wanted anything, anything else but to be a normal person. If I go ahead with this initiation ceremony, I wouldn't be normal anymore."

"I've always understood you because I want what's best for you, Charwe, because I've always known that you are someone different, that you are special. If being initiated wasn't good for you, I would've been the one to help you run away. You just have to do what the spirits require you to do. You don't have to be afraid because I will always be by your side, as I've always been."

"I'm not strong enough," Charwe told him, tears trickling down her cheeks. The man then hugged her, and she held on tight to him, wanting all his words to be true, afraid of everything that might come for her. She tried finding solace within him, but she knew one thing for a fact.

A storm was coming.

6

A Roar From The Past

At night, Chiri found himself walking to Kapfumo's hut. He had been concerned about his sister, Charwe. He looked up at the night sky, arms wrapped around his chest against the cold. The moon was full, and the stars were bright, gazing down upon him.

Chiri reached Kapfumo's hut and knocked on the door.

"Come in," he heard the answer, and he opened the door and walked in. He found Kapfumo sitting near the fire, smoking a pipe. "Feel at home, young one. You've never visited me before; I'm quite honoured to have you here."

"The Chief has been restless the whole day, since you told him about Charwe," Chiri said. "I want to understand more about this Nehanda spirit. Why does she seem so important?"

"I blame all of this on the elders nowadays," Kapfumo said. "They don't teach the children the most essential and important stories and elements of our histories. It should be an obscenity for any person to not know anything about the Mhondoro spirits, much less one of royal blood."

Chiri then sat down near the fire, across Kapfumo, so he could listen to what Kapfumo had to tell him.

"Nehanda is not just any ancestral spirit, she is a mhondoro, holding authority over any Zezuru Chief or other spirit mediums," Kapfumo said. "The mhondoro are the spirits of our first ancestors, and of the other great kings that have lived thousands of years ago. They always return through mediums during our times of great need, during our darkest of times."

"Why do you think the mhondoro has returned through our sister?"

"That is what I have been thinking about. Perhaps it is to restore our old fallen kingdom, to unite all maZezuru under one strong ruler," He replied and took out some roasted maize cob from the fire, broke it into two and threw the other half for Chiri to catch. "The mhondoro were the initial architects of Dzimbabwe after all."

"We are fine the way we are, we do not need to restore the kingdom," Chiri said, as he ate the roasted maize. "With all the craziness and differences within our different chiefdoms, I don't even think that they can ever be merged to form a single kingdom."

"We cannot continue being vassals for other great kingdoms, when we lie on the shoulders of the greatest civilisation ever known in the history of this land. The amaNdebele and all other groups out there have their own kings, kingdoms, and they have strong military forces. What do we have? We are only Sub-Chiefs, constantly quarrelling about land pieces, and at the mercy of other greater powers. We are in great need," Kapfumo said. "Nehanda might be able to restore back the fallen kingdom and return all that was lost. Yes, the great Dzimbabwe kingdom fell five centuries ago, but we all have the potential to awaken it again. We are a giant that is just asleep."

"Tell me, if the kingdom is restored again, who would ever be the ruler?" Chiri asked. "I don't think that the line of succession is still clear. Is the royal bloodline known?"

"No, it's not clear. No true heirs of the Mutapa or Rozvi Empire are still known, and we must take that to our advantage. We are the Hwata dynasty, and your older father is one of the most powerful Chiefs out there. A new line of succession would need to be formed, that's why we are lucky to have a mhondoro in our own family. A mhondoro must always be under a King and that's why we have to keep Charwe close."

Chiri had a hard time digesting what Kapfumo had told him. The Chief wanted Nehanda so that he would rise and restore the great Zezuru kingdom, so that he would be King. Well, if Gwindi would ever be the King, that would mean that Kemuteku was going to succeed him one day. They might create a new line of succession and rebuild the long destroyed kingdom. The thought of it turned Chiri's bowels, for he knew that his dear brother would never want all of that.

Kemu never wanted to be a Chief, let alone a King of a whole Kingdom. He never wanted power, or to hear anything about it.

"Thank you for the information," Chiri said and stood up. "I hope that the will of the spirits will be done, peacefully. I've to go now."

"I hope you have a pleasant night," Kapfumo smiled at Chiri as he walked out of his hut.

As Chiri ventured into the night, the moon cast a gentle glow upon his path. The air was cool and carried the whispers of the chirping crickets. It was then that Chiri noticed a familiar figure sitting alone at the edge of a nearby cliff, overlooking the landscape below.

It was his brother, Kemuteku.

Chiri approached Kemu with a soft step, his heart filled with concern. He sat down next to him, the silence between them speaking volumes. From the cliff's edge, they could see the vast expanse of green fields stretching out before them, the sparkling river meandering through the land, and the majestic Mazowe hills standing tall in the distance.

"You always come here whenever you overthink. Tell me, what are you thinking about today?" Chiri asked his brother.

Kemu sighed and looked away. "About everything. About the raids. About the dynasty. About... my future. Kapfumo told me earlier about Charwe and said that she might be able to make me a King of the lands that run from river Zambezi to Limpopo, and even beyond. I don't want it, I don't want any responsibilities, or involvement in any disputes whatsoever."

"You worry too much, brother," Chiri said. "Know that you are a Museyamwa, the great eland bull, the one who bears heavy burdens. You are a descendant of those who challenged each other at Janga, those who were given wives from Njanja."

"I feel a bit brave and proud whenever I listen to a totem praise song and want to believe that it is true but I then remember that I don't even know where Janga or Njanja are, or if those places even exist at all."

"That doesn't change the fact that you are the heir of the Hwata dynasty, that you'll lead the court one day, and that everyone will have to obey your commands."

"What if I don't want all of that, what if I don't want duty?" Kemu asked.

"Refusing your inheritance or being afraid of ruling means that you are weak, and there is only one thing that happens to people who are weak. They die." Chiri told his brother the sad truth. "It's only that we are given what we do not want, what we do not ask. Charwe never asked for anything. I know her, she wants nothing else but a normal life, without people expecting too much from her, and now she will be Nehanda, the most powerful medium ever. We all have no choice but to just dance along with the wind, just as you are dancing to it."

Chiri saw that this did not make Kemu any happier. He wrapped his arm around Kemu's shoulder and gave him a gentle squeeze. "Never forget that I'm here, I'm always here. I promise that I will always be by your side, and I will share all the burden that will come your way." Kemu smiled warmly at his brother, his eyes sparkling with tears in the moonlight.

Chiri wanted to cry, as everything was just pushing down against him. His sister was going to be a spiritualist, and she never wanted it. His brother was going to succeed their father, and he too never wanted it. The two had been chosen by their ancestors, and they never wanted the burden that came with their duties. He was their pillar. He wondered if the ancestors had planned something for him too, and he was scared to even think of what it could be.

Kemu glanced at the landscape, tears sparkling in his eyes. "It might sound crazy, but every time I close my eyes, I only see bright colours. I see myself in a forest, where I can always smile and never cry. I see myself surrounded by trees with blooming flowers of every colour, and with all the animals running free."

"It's not crazy to wish for a little bit of magic," Chiri said softly. "We all need some hope in our lives, especially when things seem uncertain."

"But why do bushes have thorns, why are there cold winters in the world?" Kemu looked up at his brother. "Why do locusts eat our crops, why does rinderpest kill our cattle, why do we have a drought? If the creator and the spirits love us so much, why is there suffering in this world?"

"I honestly don't know," Chiri told his brother. "But I do know that beauty exists, if you search far enough. Hidden underneath this horrible suffering on earth, there are trees with blooming flowers and animals that run free. We get hurt but wounds heal. People die and wake up to live as powerful spirits. There are still people in this world who care about each other, just like you and me."

Kemu looked at Chiri with a smile, "Like you." Chiri returned his smile and looked also at the landscape.

He was smiling but he could only think about what Charwe had told him, about her dream, and it instilled fear within him. A storm was coming, and he could only wonder if Kemu would be strong enough to survive through it.

7

The Initiation Ceremony

When the first rays of morning painted the sky with multiple hues of gold, Chief Gwindi, accompanied by Chiri, Kemu, Meda and Muti, made their way to Charwe's homestead. The air was filled with anticipation as the villagers gathered, their voices harmonising in ceremonial songs, preparing for Charwe's initiation ceremony. Everyone was happy and cheerful, for they all had been told that a very powerful spirit had arrived to make them as rich as kings and queens once more.

However, Charwe was conspicuously absent from the crowd.

"I tried to convince her to join us," Kapfumo explained this to Chief Gwindi with a sympathetic tone. "But poor Charwe is still overcome with nervousness. She truly does not wish to undergo the initiation."

Chief Gwindi's face tightened with determination. "We cannot afford to delay any longer," he declared firmly. "Inform Charwe that her chief commands her presence and expects her to fulfil her duties as the spirits require her. She must understand the significance of this ceremony."

Sensing the Chief's impatience, Chiri stepped forward, then turned to Meda, and gave him a command. "Go and speak to her. Persuade her to come and join us for her ceremony."

"Me?" Meda hesitated, confused. "How can I..."
Chiri moved closer and placed his hand on Meda's shoulder.

"Make haste, Meda. The people wait."

With no other choice, Meda gave a nod, then set off towards Charwe's hut, trying to find the right words to tell her.

As he reached her door, he paused for a moment, gathering his thoughts, before gently pushing it open. Inside, Charwe stood with her arms folded, taking slow and deep breaths, trying to calm herself.

Charwe's eyes widened when she saw Meda standing in the doorway. Her heart raced, pounding against her chest.

"Mangwanani," Meda walked to Charwe. "Chiri sent me. They are all waiting for you outside, for your ceremony."

He extended his hand to her, his expression gentle. Charwe's breath caught in her throat.

Charwe wanted to hold his hand, to touch his skin for the first time, but she knew that he was taking her out there.

"No," she shook her head, her voice trembling. "I'm afraid to walk out there."
Meda moved closer, his hand still outstretched. When he took hers, his grip was firm, offering reassurance. "You don't

need to be afraid, Charwe. I don't know much but they say you'll become Nehanda, that you'll be powerful. Come with me. They need you out there. I will be right here beside you, every step of the way. Together, we will face the unknown, and nothing will harm you as long as I am by your side."

The warmth of his hand began to soothe her nerves, calming the storm inside her. She looked into his eyes, finding them impossibly perfect, and wondering how he made her the way she felt. Taking a deep breath, she tightened her grip on his hand, drawing strength from his touch.

Why was she so drawn to him? She had always admired him from a distance, never daring to get too close. With him holding her hand, they walked slowly towards the door, her pulse quickening with each step. Beads of sweat formed on her forehead, as she had been fighting many battles in her mind.

"Stay strong," Meda whispered, his voice a soothing balm to her anxious soul.

Did he ever know that all this time she had been longing to hear his voice close to her?

Meda then swung the door open, revealing a scene beyond Charwe's wildest expectations. The air filled with joyous ululations and thunderous applause, echoing through the gathering. The crowd was larger than Charwe had imagined.

"They've all travelled from far and wide, just to see you," Meda told her. "You are their guardian spirit, something special to them."

As she walked through the villagers, hand in hand with Meda, they all beheld Charwe with awe and reverence, their eyes filled with expectations of what she was going to become.

Meda had told her that he believed that she was something special to them. She wanted to share that same belief but deep within, she felt a tremor of vulnerability, a sensation she had never experienced before. Meda should've felt her grip tightening on his hand. Fear coursed through Charwe's veins, reminding her that she stood at the precipice of an unknown destiny.

As the weight of the impending initiation ceremony pressed upon her, she couldn't help but question her place in this grand scheme. Was she ever going to control the events that would soon unfold in her life? The path ahead seemed daunting and uncertain, shrouded in a haze of mystery.

Her gaze shifted to Chiri, who was standing next to her older father, the esteemed Gwindi Goredema. Kemu and Muti were also standing by Chiri's side.

Chiri offered her a smile. She did not return his smile. He was the one that had sent for Meda to get her. She wanted to hate him for that, though she couldn't.

The villagers were there to witness this initiation ceremony, unaware of Charwe's inner turmoil.

Charwe took a deep breath, summoning the remnants of her courage. Though her heart pounded, she vowed to face the challenges ahead with resilience. She had no other choice. There was no going back. She knew that this initiation ceremony would forever change her, moulding her into something different, something she never really knew.

Meda escorted her to the circle, where Kapfumo had been waiting for her.

There had been a wall of stones around the circle, and a goatskin mat in the middle. The multitudes stood around the circle, as they watched her walking into it.

As Meda's hand slipped from hers, she turned to him, feeling as though he was abandoning her. He then gave her a nod, silently telling her that there was nothing to fear.

"Sit on the mat, with your legs crossed," Kapfumo instructed Charwe. The smell of snuff on Kapfumo irritated her nostrils.

She would soon be a medium herself, and she knew she had to get used to the smell of the snuff. From that day onwards, snuff and millet beer were going to be her life. Every spiritualist must always have those things with them.

Charwe looked at the mat, and it seemed very new. In her ears, she could hear the bleating sound of the goat that had been killed and ripped from its skin.

"It's not death, but rebirth," Kapfumo whispered to Charwe, as if he had been reading her mind. "You will still be Nyakasikana, and you will still have your consciousness and your memories."

I don't want to, Charwe wanted to say, but she found herself taking a step on the mat. With one last glance at Meda, Charwe lowered herself onto the mat, bracing herself for whatever was to come. She could feel the furs of the goat on her own skin. A spiritualist interacts in two worlds, the one where Nyakasikana lived, and the one where the goat had found a new home.

A calabash of millet beer was then given to her, so that she could take a sip. With little choice, she had nothing else to do other than to take a sip from the calabash. She never liked the smell nor the taste of beer. It was too sour for her tongue.

Kapfumo took the calabash, and also drank from it.

Charwe then turned to the other villagers, who had already started dancing and singing. The mbira players and the drummers joined in, commencing her ceremony. A cloud of dust rose as they shook the rattle shakers on their legs.

All those people had been singing and dancing, only for her. They had left their homes just for this ceremony, just for her.

It's all beginning, she thought in her mind. Her initiation ceremony had truly begun.

"*Mhondoro dzinomwa muna Save*," the people sang.

"Listen to the music, flow with it, just surrender your whole being to it," Kapfumo instructed her. "You will feel your inner self awakening. Drink from Save, the great river. Drink from the river of memories, of the old lives that once belonged to you. Drink, drink from the river of the Mhondoro, keep on drinking, do not stop."

Charwe never tried listening to the music, but she could feel it, all the tension building in the air.

Everything was slowly shifting, changing the world around her. She was slowly drifting away, making a journey to a whole new world, all in her mind.

Each key of the mbira was like a voice calling unto her, calling her name. The drums were her very heart, pounding new life within her. Her veins seemed to have ears of their own, and the blood in her seemed to dance along.

She just sat down, not moving, but she could feel herself dancing, her arms and legs moving, her voice singing to the songs. She could even feel the wind around her dancing.

Charwe could hear voices in her head, along with thundering storms. Memories and visions flashed in her mind, as the whole world spun around her.

"No, I can't do this," she told Kapfumo. "I'm afraid."

"It's good to be afraid, your power will give you the strength you need," Kapfumo told her. "Close your eyes and seek out that power, that courage."

"Don't worry, everything will be fine," Chiri whispered to her.

As soon as she closed her eyes, all the music and singing started drifting away. She felt herself falling deeper into a world that had always been hidden in her mind.

Don't worry, everything will be fine.

She then found herself all alone, standing on a hilltop, looking at the vast landscape. Her name was Nehanda and that was the first thing she remembered as she stood on that hilltop.

It had been her first time standing on that hilltop, but it felt as familiar as her mother's hut, and the embrace of her mother's arms.

She then realised that she was not in the waking world anymore. Something had taken her from the world she had grown and known, to this strange place she had never seen before, yet it was more familiar than the world that she had grown up in and known.

A man then appeared in front of her, the one who had always been there, and the one who will always be there. He was the man from her dreams, Murenga Pfumojena Sororenzou. This time, there was no mist around them, and she could see everything clearly.

She was standing atop a hill, and there were three other boys standing alongside her.

It was the first time she saw their faces but it seemed as if she had known them for a very long time, more than she knew her own mother. She was standing with her other brothers, sons of Murenga.

It was the music that had drifted her mind into this world which felt as real as the one she had left.

"Upon this soil, we shall create our kingdom, as strong as Mapungubwe had been," she heard the man saying.

"You all, the four of you, shall be the guardians of that great kingdom. You are my children, you are the fearless mhondoro spirits, and your roars shall reach the far ends of the land. You must protect it to the very end, like a lion protects its pride. Do you hear me?"

"Yes father," one of the boys replied.

At that moment, Charwe found herself falling again, now drifting back to the music and the singing voices. She knew that she was now returning to the waking world.

As soon as she could, she reopened her eyes, and found herself back at her homestead, where people had been singing and dancing.

She felt as if she had been undrowning herself from a bottomless river, and her heart pounded so hard, in her ears and she found it to be as loud as the drums.

Charwe gathered her thoughts and tried to think of what had happened. Where had she gone to?

She had been standing with Murenga and his sons, people that had lived thousands of years ago. She then joined all the dots together and realised it all. She had just revisited a memory of her past life, of her incarnate, the first Nehanda.

Kapfumo, realising that Charwe had returned to the waking world, helped her to stand up, then raised his hand, and the music halted. Everyone was still and quiet and Charwe realised that they wanted to hear what she had to say.

"Walk forward and talk to your people," Kapfumo told her. "You've been initiated; you now have the spirit within you. They want to hear from you, their Mhondoro."

Charwe never wanted to talk. She never knew she had the energy to do so.

"What should I say to them?" she asked him.

"They want confirmation. Tell them who you really are," Kapfumo said, as he moved backwards, so the people might pay more attention to her, rather than him.

Charwe still was afraid. She turned to Chiri, and he nodded slightly at her, though she could see a bit of unease within him, something unusual.

Kapfumo had told her to tell them who she was. She was Nyakasikana Charwe, a normal daughter under the chieftainship of Hwata Gwindi, a normal girl who just wanted a normal life.

Yes, she had been Nyakasikana Charwe, but her vision had shown her that she was something else other than Nyakasikana Charwe. That something else was what the people had been waiting to hear.

She didn't want to confirm to them that she truly was Nehanda. She knew that the responsibility that came with that title was so large as to shake the world. It was not only the responsibility, but it was her very life. She would have to leave Nyakasikana behind and wear the face of Nehanda.

As much as she wanted to run away from the fact that she was Nehanda, she knew that she was never going to be able to get away with it. This was her life, her destiny.

She had to just tell them who she really was. Charwe Nyakasikana gathered up her strength and took a deep breath.

"I am Nehanda, the great Mhondoro, daughter of Murenga, and guardian spirit of the Zezuru dynasty," she confirmed to the people, then went on to tell them what she had seen in her vision.

The people smiled when they heard her words. The women ululated and the men clapped their hands as they whistled.

She turned to Meda and saw him smiling at her. As much as she could remember, this was probably the first time she saw him smiling at her.

Chiri saw the two smiling at one another, and he felt good. He walked to Charwe, then whispered to her. "You did good. You spoke with great confidence."

No, she wasn't really as confident as she should be, and she knew it. Nehanda was a lion spirit, and she had to walk and speak with great confidence, like she knew she had sharp claws and teeth. Her voice was to roar, and all that heard it had to tremble.

More than ever, she knew she had to be strong. The responsibility that had fallen on her shoulders was no child's play. She was a leader of the Zezuru, a broken people.

Their territories had moved further from one another, and they had developed different accents, even different social structures.

The different chiefs were even said to be greedy and quarrelled among themselves over land pieces and territory lines.

The Chief, Hwata Gwindi, then went on his knees and clapped his hands.

"I'm the Chief of this land, great one," he said before her, as his men brought a black cow to her, as per tradition. "We welcome you with open arms. This is the meat with which we greet you."

Nehanda Charwe Nyakasikana accepted the cow, as expected. She was nervous and anxious at the same time, for she knew a fact.

A storm was coming.

8

The Pool named Peace

Charwe sat quietly in her rondavel hut, staring into the flickering flames of the fire. She had been thinking about the initiation ceremony. It was already dark outside, and the crickets had already started their nightly chorus.

The door creaked open, and she turned to see her son, Hungwariri, stepping inside. He had returned from Chenge's village.

"Mother," he greeted her, then walked closer. "I heard about the ceremony, that you are now someone else, Nehanda."

"What do you think?" she asked, and looked right at him, curious to hear what he had to say.

He shook his head, his eyes filled with confusion and worry. "I don't know. What are you now?"

A slight smile tugged at her lips. "What kind of question is that? It was just a ceremony, nothing more. I'm Charwe, your mother. Do I seem like I'm something else now?"

"I don't think it's just a ceremony," he told her, tears glowing in his eyes. "Everyone out there is talking about it, and I, your firstborn son, was the last to know. You didn't even want me to be part of it. You tried sending me away. Do you know how scared I was, thinking I was going to come here, and see that you are no longer my mother."

She walked over to him and gently cupped his cheek. "No, Hungwa, you don't understand. I did not try sending you away because of that. There are other things at play here."

"What other things?" he asked, his lower lip trembling.

"My dreams," Charwe replied softly, pulling him into a hug. "Something big is coming, something dangerous. I don't know what it is yet, but I feel like I'm meant to face it and stop it from destroying all of you."

Just then, a knock came at the door.

"Come in," Charwe called, turning towards the entrance. Chief Gwindi walked in with Chiri by his side. Hungwa looked down, so that his chief might not see the tears that were threatening to spill from his eyes.

"Good evening, Charwe," Gwindi said with a smile. "How was your day?"

"Not too bad," she replied, forcing a smile. "I hope yours was good as well."

"It was," Gwindi said. "I'm glad to hear that yours was good. I want to inform you that there will be a rainmaking ceremony tomorrow. The other spiritualists have tried, but the heavens have stayed grim. Perhaps you, a mhondoro, can shift the winds. Also, word of your initiation has been spread across the land. Soon enough, chiefs will start arriving at court just to see you."

Charwe's smile faltered. She was not yet ready for the attention.

Gwindi then turned to Hungwa. "Your son seems quite grown," he remarked. "I'm heading to Mthwakazi tomorrow to meet with the king. It's a long journey. I'll need someone to escort me."

Hungwa looked at his mother, uncertain. He didn't want to go away from her again.

He agreed, driven by respect for the chief, but he couldn't shake the feeling that they were trying to distance him from his mother.

He then excused himself and walked out of the room.

"If you are going to Mthwakazi tomorrow, who is going to stay behind and lead the rainmaking ceremony?" she asked her chief.

"That would be you, and Kemuteku. He will be acting chief when I'm gone," Gwindi said. "I wanted to lead the ceremony myself, but I cannot, time is not on my side. I've to resolve this issue with Mthwakazi as soon as I can."

Charwe turned to Chiri, as if trying to silently ask him if he agreed with all of this. He did not say anything, but just stared back at her.

"There is something else," Chief Gwindi told her. "To secure ourselves from any future raids, I have a plan to unite all the other chiefdoms under the Hwata arm, and your influence as a mhondoro can be pivotal. I want you to be part of it."

"I don't understand," Charwe shook her head, seemingly confused.

"You are a mhondoro, Charwe," he told her. "You command respect and have the power to change our future. Whatever you say or do, every other chief will follow. You can speak the wishes of the creator himself."

"No," Charwe shook her head, not wanting all that was being thrown at her. "I don't want to be part of any plans of yours. I never even wanted to go on with this initiation, and now you are piling things on me. I never wanted anything, only a normal life, only peace of mind. If you wish to pursue your conquests, do so without me."

She walked out of her room, to go somewhere where she would be alone. She wanted to go to the cliff overlooking the mountains, but she knew that might be where her son was. He needed his own space, she thought.

She then decided to climb up Shavarudzi hill and walked to the graves of all the previous chiefs. The night was thick with shadows, and as she drew nearer, she noticed a figure moving in the dark. Her heart skipped a beat when she realised who it was.

"Meda?" she whispered, startled. "What are you doing here?"

"I might ask you the same question, Nehanda," he replied.

Even though it was dark, there was always something about his eyes, something that unsettled her.

"I'm not yet used to that name," Charwe admitted, trying to steady her voice. "I may be Nehanda, but I still feel the same as before. Nothing's really changed."

"Nothing should change, I think," Meda said, stepping closer. "You were always Nehanda, from the day you were born."

Charwe swallowed hard, noticing that he was close to her. "You still haven't answered my question."

"I come here often, when I feel like I want to talk with the spirits," he told her.

"Can you hear them?" Charwe asked him.

"No," he shook his head. "I'm not a spiritualist like you."

I don't hear the spirits, Charwe wanted to say, though she stayed quiet because she knew what her dreams were.

"You seemed very nervous at the ceremony," Meda said gently.

He tried looking right into her eyes, and she moved her eyes away, her heart pacing. His eyes were just the same brown as everyone else. What was it about those eyes of his?

"Why did you come to get me?" she asked. She had been wondering about that the whole day.

"I was just given an order to get you," Meda told her. "Or perhaps I knew that you were someone special, a medium of the guardian spirit of our people. At least that is what everyone else is saying."

"There is nothing really special about me," Charwe murmured. "I'm just Charwe. Nothing more."

"Why have you come here?" he asked her.

"I don't know," she admitted. "I just felt like I needed to be here, away from everyone else. I think I came here because I needed peace."

"Perhaps it was the wind that guided you," Meda said, a small smile playing on his lips.

"This hill is said to be sacred, Nehanda."

"My name is Charwe. I don't hear anything in the wind," Charwe replied, shaking her head.

Meda's smile grew, then turned and started walking away. "Come. Walk with me."

"I do not wish—"

"I need to show you something."

Charwe hesitated, then she walked to catch up with him. He walked in front, stepping over fallen branches.

"Why do you turn away?" he asked suddenly, his tone serious.

"What are you talking about?" Charwe's voice was shaky.

"At court," Meda said, glancing over his shoulder. "You always turn away whenever I look at you."

"No, I don't," she said, as a shiver ran down her spine.

As she walked, he stretched his hand out to hold her from stepping farther. A cliff, though the drop was not far.

"There is a pool here," she was surprised as she looked at the still and blue water under the moonlight . She never knew that there was ever a pool on Shavarudzi hill.

"It's sacred," Meda told her quietly. "I once looked deep into it, and I saw your face's reflection. All this time, I was trying to figure out what it truly meant. But now I know."

"You saw my face?" Charwe was shocked. "When was this?"

He looked right at her, and it amused him to see how seriously shocked she had been. He then chuckled at her. "I'm just playing, Nehanda. No need to be so serious about it. I never saw any reflections. I told you that I'm not a spiritualist, even though I'm curious to know how it feels to be one."

"That was not very funny," she said, a frown on her face. "And you are the one who is always serious. You hardly speak at court."

"Why should I try talking in those droning sessions?" he said. "They always quarrel over the same issues every day."

The night hid her smile, and she was glad for it. She then turned her gaze back at the pool. "Do you really believe that this pool is sacred?"

Meda then walked into the pool and moved his legs swiftly as he floated above the pool, his gaze up at the moon. "I always swim in this pool. In my mind, I imagine that I'm not alone. I imagine that I'm in this pool, swimming with the spirits of those who've been gone for so very long."

Charwe looked right at him. "Do you really believe that I am sacred?"

"I believe all women are sacred," Meda replied. "They bring life to the world. To raise your hand on a woman is to curse yourself. There was a man in my village who beat his mother, Taku. Since she died, he has been roaming from village to village in ash and rags, running and shouting, cursed with madness."

Charwe watched him, feeling a strange mixture of admiration and warmth. "Why did you bring me here," she asked him.

"Do you know that this pool is named Peace," he said. "This is what you wanted, right? You said you came here for peace. Jump in."

Charwe laughed. "You are mad if you think that I'm going to follow you into that cold pool."

"You haven't even touched the water," he said with a grin. "How are you so sure that it is cold?"

"You are Nehanda?" he continued. "If you fear that it's cold, perhaps you can give the command and then it will be warm."

Charwe couldn't help but smile, finding it hard to believe that this was the same quiet, mysterious man from court.

"I think I need to go back home," she said, as she turned around.

"What? Nehanda. Just imagine this. I am attacked by a mermaid. She wants to drown me so that I can become her servant. You must come and save me from her. You know what they say about men taken by mermaids. She will feed me worms down there. Come save me. Nehanda, I will not stop shouting your name until you do. Nehanda, do you wish to see me gone from court forever? Nehanda! Nehanda!"

She then stopped and turned around with frustration. "Can you please just stop calling me that name?"

He laughed. "Why not, Nehanda Nyakasikana?"

She just shook her head, with a smile dancing at her lips. She then turned around and continued walking away.

"Are you seriously going to let the mermaid take me!" he asked her, even though he was now talking alone. "Nehanda, come back!"

She was already gone.

9

Mukwerera

Charwe walked beside her two brothers, Chiri and Kemu, as they made their way towards Shavarudzi.

She glanced at Kemu and could see that he was just as nervous as her. With the chief gone, he was going to lead the ceremony with her.

Charwe found herself thinking about her three children who were all far away. Hungwariri had gone south with the Chief, and her other two children were at her sister's place. She assured herself that they were all safe and far from harm.

The ground beneath their feet shifted, demanding their full attention. The air was crisp and thin, making every breath feel like a struggle.

"I don't know if I will ever get used to people seeing me as their leader," Kemu spoke, as they walked. "I know that I'm not as strong as is expected of a Hwata heir."

Chiri, his face flushed with exertion, offered a comforting smile. "Don't worry, maybe you'll get used to it as time goes on."

Charwe let out a weary sigh. "No one can ever get used to chaos, dear Chiri," she said, her voice tinged with sadness. "I know how it feels. There is chaos in my mind too. Part of me wants to be this Nehanda, and part of me doesn't."

As they uttered their words, the distant sound of singing reached their ears, carried by the wind. Soft at first, the melodic tunes grew louder with each step, like a chorus of voices climbing alongside them. The villagers had gathered at the shrine, their ceremonial songs filling the air with anticipation and reverence.

Charwe took a deep breath, before walking through the gathering, to stand near the graves. The voices of the villagers grew louder, their chants resonating through the sacred space, as she was handed a clay pot filled with fermenting beer.

She prayed that no one saw the way she scrawled her face with disgust. She couldn't even guess what the little things floating on top of the beer were.

She closed her eyes, then gathered her strength, and raised the pot to her lips. The liquid was warm, and when she took a sip, she felt a surge of energy flow through her. She had never liked beer, all her life, until that very moment. That fact alone proved to her that she was not the same as before the initiation.

Charwe lifted her head, and turned around, looking for Meda, but he was not there, at the ceremony. She looked at the trees in the distance and wondered if he had been in the pool named Peace.

She had been twisting and turning the whole night, thinking of why she had not followed him into the pool.

Charwe handed the cup to her brothers who took turns to sip the beer. Kemu had wanted to pretend as if he had taken a sip, but then noticed that Chiri was looking to see if he really drank it. The acting Chief coughed as the sour taste of the beer seeped in his mouth.

Charwe then walked towards the graves of past chiefs and knelt before them. The mbira players surrounding her started plucking their instruments, and she began to clap her hands rhythmically.

She closed her eyes and began to chant in a low voice, invoking the names of the ancestors and asking them to tell the creator to bring down the rain, just as Kapfumo had instructed her.

She felt a warm breeze on her skin, and a faint smell of smoke, though there had been nothing burning.

The mbira always invoked something within her, some energy that simply sprouted from nowhere. As she clapped her hands, she felt herself flowing with the wind, flowing somewhere else, somewhere new. Everything went quiet, then after a while, she heard mumbling voices.

Charwe opened her eyes and realised that she was in one of her visions.

She was standing in a yard surrounded by a circular wall of stones piled one over the other. The yard was filled with people: men, women, children, old and young, and they were all looking directly at her.

Who were they? Where were they? Why were they looking at her?

The King of that place was also standing with the people, along with all the royal officials. It was easy to know, for they had been standing at the front, dressed in elegant and colourful dresses, adorned with golden jewellery that shone in the sunlight.

She thought they were looking at her, then realised that it had been something else behind her. She then turned and saw a young girl standing on a raised platform.

The girl was lean and young, with the defiant face of a warrior. She was very beautiful, with jet black hair that sat behind her head like a black sun. She had a spiral *ndoro* amulet tied around her forehead.

The name of this young girl was then heralded for all. "Behold the Princess, Nehanda Nyamhita of the Heart totem, daughter of Nyatsimba Mutota, and granddaughter of the great king Chibatamatosi. Behold your Mhondoro, the vessel of the great lion spirit of this land."

Charwe then turned back to the people and realised that their gaze had been focused on that girl and not her. It seemed as if they couldn't even see her.

The mbira players started plucking their instruments, and everyone in the enclosure went quiet, to hear what Nyamhita had to say.

"I do not bring pleasant tidings," the girl said. "I had a terrible dream about the future. I found myself standing by the shores of a vast lake. I saw strange kneeless men emerging from the water. I saw them spreading throughout the land like locusts. They were digging the ground like meerkats. I saw darkness falling upon the land, then heard voices of men singing war songs and the women screaming. The stars in the night sky turned into a thousand spears raining over villages, striking men and cattle alike. The spears turned to a fire that burned forests and villages, destroying everything."

Gasps and whispers rose from the crowds, but they quickly died out to silence, as the people wanted to hear more from their Mhondoro. Charwe also gasped, as that was exactly what she had seen in her own dreams.

"When the kneeless men come, even if it's in a thousand years, I, Nehanda, your great Mhondoro, swear that I will return to stand and fight with the people, my people," she said.

In the blink of an eye, everything turned to mist, then to darkness, and her consciousness returned to her.

She was back at Shavarudzi, surrounded by the Hwata people performing the rain-making ceremony.

Charwe, still reeling from the unsettling vision, struggled to maintain her composure as she continued with the ceremony. She took deep breaths, trying to think about what had happened. She had seen another Nehanda in the vision, glanced into her own past. She already knew about this dream of the kneeless men back then.

Chiri could also notice that Charwe's demeanour had changed. He observed her distant gaze and the furrowed lines on her forehead. Her mind was clouded with thoughts of what the vision really meant. She couldn't shake off the feeling that something ominous loomed on the horizon, something about those kneeless men.

"How are you feeling, Charwe?" Chiri asked Charwe after she had done her rites.

"I think I know," she looked straight into his eyes, increasingly distressed. "I think I know the reason why the spirit of Nehanda has returned through me. A storm is coming with the kneeless men."

"The kneeless men? You mean the Europeans?" Chiri asked.

"Men shall sing war songs and women shall scream," Nehanda said, seemingly very much afraid. "Stars shall rain down and villages shall burn."

"I never thought that the Europeans posed any danger," he said. "They all seem like decent traders."

"I have to find out more about them, they are the reason why I'm here," Nehanda told him. At that moment, a groan of thunder sounded, and they all turned up to the sky.

The crowd, momentarily stilled, looked skyward. Fat, rain-laden clouds had gathered, promising a much-needed downpour. Cheers erupted throughout the gathering, celebrating the successful ceremony.

Chiri grinned at Charwe, his eyes sparkling. "You did it, Charwe! You are a true lioness, powerful indeed."

Her smile, weak and fleeting, couldn't quite reach her eyes. Her gaze fixed on the ominous clouds, worry etched deep into her face. She could clearly see through them.

A raindrop splattered onto Charwe's cheek, mimicking the tear she was trying to hold back. The cheers of the crowd felt hollow now. She glanced at Chiri, her expression etched with worry despite the smattering of rain on her skin.

"We should brace ourselves for a great famine, Chiri," Charwe's low voice warned. "We must all be strong from now on."

"What do you mean?" he asked her. "You are Nehanda, you are a rainmaker."

"I am, but prophecy is prophecy, and fate is fate," she told him. "Nothing can ever change anything. It all awaits to be fulfilled."

The clouds above roared, and it started raining.

Charwe watched the villagers singing songs of praise as they descended Shavarudzi hill to return to their villages. Charwe knew that their songs would not last long, and that feeling was tormenting her.

She remained behind, for she needed nothing more than peace. She turned around and could feel it calling unto her. Chiri wanted to stay behind with her, but she gently told him that she wanted to be alone.

She turned, and she walked past the graves to the pool. Lit by the moonlight that peeped from the dark clouds, she saw Meda swimming in the pool.

He smiled when he saw her, all soaked up in the rain of her own making. "I knew you would come back."

"Is it not disrespectful to the spirits to be absent from a rainmaking ceremony?" she asked, her voice tinged with both curiosity and reproach.

"How could I have come when you left the mermaid to drown me?" he replied, looking up at the water pouring down on him. "Yesterday, you asked if I believed you were sacred. To be honest, I don't think I ever truly believed."

"I didn't believe in myself when I asked you that question," she admitted as he walked out of the pool, coming closer to her. "I never believed that I could be..." Her words faltered as he moved too close, his breath warm against her face.

He gazed into her eyes, and she fought hard not to look away, feeling a flutter of nerves in her chest.

"Shall I call you by the name you asked me not to use?" he murmured, his breath brushing her skin. Without waiting for her reply, he whispered, "Nehanda," and gently lifted her chin, pressing his lips to hers in the rain.

10

The god of the Sun and the Moon

Nehanda Charwe walked from her hut out into the sunlight, the smell of the after rain making her smile.

Chiri had been waiting for her outside with his usual smile. "You look too bright today, Charwe Nyakasikana. You have a visitor at court who wishes to speak with you."

"Do you know who the visitor is?" she asked him, as they started walking their way to court.

"Chief Matope," Chiri told her. "He said that he has travelled far just to see you. He also says he has precious gifts for you."

Nehanda Charwe smiled. Chiri noticed that she was unusually bright that day, but did not care to ask her, for she knew the reason. He had seen her the previous night, walking from Shavarudzi with Meda.

As they walked into the court, their visitor went up on his feet, and his gaze landed on Charwe.

"I am Chief Matope, the god of the sun and the moon," he quickly introduced himself to her.

The man was very handsome, and wore a golden elegant robe, with matching rings, bangles and chains.

"The god of the sun and the moon?" She was a bit confused.

"Yes. Like you, I am a direct descendant of Mutapa Matope, son of the great Nyatsimba Mutota," he explained himself. "I inherited his name, thus I also inherited the title that his subjects addressed him with."

"Why did they call him the god of the sun and the moon?" she asked him.

"I must admit, I do not know," he told her. "Much of the tales of the Mutapa kings have been lost in time. One might think they are just mere myths. Tales of wars, legends and the Mhondoro. Who would ever know that a Mhondoro will ever walk on the soil after five hundred years? Tell me, why have you returned after so long?"

Charwe could also see through his soft smile, he also had a golden tooth. She took a moment to gather her thoughts before she replied to him.

"That's precisely what I'm trying to unravel," she explained. "I believe it has something to do with the new traders in the region, the Europeans. That's why I'm eager to hear your thoughts on them, Chief Matope."

A smug grin spread across the Chief's face. "Ah, the Europeans. They are not just good friends; they are the epitome of reliability. Their trading skills are unparalleled, and their craftsmanship is simply extraordinary."

He ran his hand down his elegant and golden robe, which had an intricate tapestry woven into its surface. "This exquisite piece is a gift from their administrator, Leander Starr Jameson, a token of his appreciation for my unwavering loyalty. Look closely, and you'll see the fine details that showcase their unmatched skill and intelligence."

"Unwavering loyalty?" Chiri could not understand.

"Our relations have grown quite intimate," Matope explained, with his usual exotic accent. "They mine their gold and acquire small pieces of land. In return, they spoil us with gifts and offer us their protection."

"Do you not think that might be of concern?" Charwe asked him. "Should we not fear them?"

"No, we shouldn't, only our enemies," he smiled. "Right now as we speak, they are mounting an assault on our arch-nemesis, the Matabele Kingdom, as vengeance for the execution of Chief Gomora, another loyal patron. Soon enough the Ndebele Military Kingdom will be nothing other than history."

"What do you mean they are marching an assault on the AmaNdebele? Are they not overreaching themselves?" Chiri asked.

Nehanda fought to calm herself, though within her, a fear grew. Her firstborn son, her dear Hungwariri, had gone with Chief Hwata to the kingdom of the AmaNdebele. She wondered if her boy was safe.

"You should take this as good news dear friend," Chief Matope said. "The Europeans are helping us, and they don't even want anything more in return, just gold."

"What do you mean, just gold? That mineral is much more precious than you will ever know," Chiri told him. "The majesty of the old kingdom of Dzimbabwe depended on it."

"We have a lot of it, more than we need. They can never finish all the gold that is in our mountains and our rivers," Matope then turned to Nehanda. "What about you, Nehanda, maybe you have a bit more sense than this brother of yours. What do you think, which side do we take? The Matebele who raid us and demand tribute, or the traders, who give us gifts and offer their protection."

"I don't know what to think about them, but I know for a fact that they are strangers. If you are in a good relationship with them, maybe it isn't really a bad thing," Charwe spoke. "Don't be afraid of them as they are only traders but take a black cow to them and say this is the meat with which we greet you. But if they are not just traders, if they are settlers, and if they come with rules and conditions, then you've every reason to be afraid of them."

"These people are different from Matebele. They can be settlers and still be good people. There is no need to fear or repel them," Matope said. "Maybe Chief Mashayamombe has fed you with the lies about them already, telling you that they have bad intentions and that they must be driven off this land."

"Do not forget, there is a lot that can be hidden beneath a smile," Charwe told him. "These Europeans are new to us. We do not know their true intentions. Maybe there are some things Mashayamombe might know that you might not."

Matope furrowed his brows, seemingly bothered by her words.

"Is this the reason why you think you've returned? If that's the reason, I'm afraid that you are wrong," Chief Matope assured her. "After the Matebele capital falls, they will match against Mashayamombe and all the stupid chiefs that think they can repel them. They are going to crush them like the ants they are."

"Do you happen to know the reason for my return, dear Matope?" Charwe looked right into his eyes.

"I am a direct descendant of the Mutapa royal line. It can't be a coincidence that the god of the Sun and the Moon, and a Mhondoro meet up again, in five hundred years. Our alliance can restore our people's dynasty just like both our namesakes did. I'm sure there is no better reason for your return. Let us restore the Shona dynasty to its former glory."

"Then I'm afraid you are the one that is wrong," Nehanda Charwe told him. "You might bear the name of Matope but you are not him, and you know nothing about him. You are neither a god nor a Mwenemutapa."

"You are not the real Nehanda then!" Matope spoke, then he spat on the ground, and left.

After Matope left, Nehanda turned to Chiri, looking concerned. "We have to go to Mashayamombe's village and meet him, as soon as we can. I need to know what he thinks about these traders. He might have the answers I need. A storm is coming, and I hope we aren't too late to prepare."

11

The Farewell

Chiri had been searching tirelessly for Kemuteku throughout the village, as he had wanted to bid him farewell. Finally, he spotted Kemu standing by the royal Kraal, his gaze fixed upon the cattle.

Chiri approached him, sensing the sadness that enveloped Kemu's demeanour.

As Chiri stood next to Kemu, only a heavy silence, and a distant mooing of cows hung in the air, leaving both of them unsure of what to say. The wind whispered through the grass, carrying with it the earthy scent of cattle dung, along with Kemu's' unspoken fears.

"We've suffered great losses, Kemu. The rinderpest and the raids have spared us no mercy," Chiri said, wanting to break the tension.

Kemu turned to face Chiri, his eyes reflecting a mixture of sadness and reluctance. "I don't wish you to go," he confessed, his voice tinged with a hint of desperation. A cow mooed after him, as if echoing his own plea.

Chiri placed a comforting hand on Kemu's shoulder. "We will only be gone for a few days," he reassured Kemu, his voice filled with sincerity. "There are things we must inquire about, suspicions that Charwe has expressed. It's important for us to seek the truth, for the sake of our people."

Kemuteku nodded, his eyes still clouded with uncertainty. "But what if something happens while you're away? What if I need you?"

"Nothing will ever happen to you. You are the Acting Chief, they will all listen to you no matter what they might think, or what they might want. If it's the court sessions, I assure you that you can handle it all; you just have to have a little faith and believe in yourself. You have Shayachimwe's blood in your veins, Kemu. His spirit is also with you, along with those of a thousand other ancestors standing behind you. You'll have Kapfumo and the other advisors to help you."

"I'm jealous of Charwe," Kemuteku said, as he wiped the tears on his cheeks. "You'll always be by her side, and not by mine. Anyway, I will pray for your quick return, I have to do my duties, and you'll have yours to do. I will keep in mind what you've always taught me."

"I'm sorry that I'm leaving you, but this is only for a little while," Chiri told him. "When I return, I will always be by your side, I assure you. I want you to take care of yourself while I'm gone and be the Museyamwa that you are. You have the power within you to overcome any challenge that comes your way."

"I wish I was as strong as you are, brother," Kemu said. "And yet I'm the first heir of the Hwata dynasty."

"No, I'm not any different from you, I'm not that strong," Chiri replied, looking into Kemu's eyes. "I just try my best to pretend that I am. You have to remember what I always tell you."

Kemu completed Chiri's sentence, saying the words they both knew so well, "The people only see the mask you wear, not the face beneath it."

Chiri smiled. "Yes, exactly," he said, his voice full of encouragement. "And you must try your best to pretend. Show them all that you are the Chief they must respect. You are destined to lead, Kemuteku, and I will be right beside you every step of the way."

"Maybe it's easier to run away than to wear a mask," Kemu said softly, his voice tinged with vulnerability. His eyes wandered, gazing at the distant hills as if searching for solace. "Run to a place where you don't need to pretend to be something that you are not. You just be yourself, and you don't care about other people's thoughts or judgments."

Chiri's gaze softened, and he sighed, feeling the weight of his brother's words. "I understand why you feel that way, Kemu," Chiri said, his voice filled with empathy. "But running away won't solve anything. True strength lies in facing our fears and embracing the challenges that come our way. There's no perfect world out there. If you are weak, you'll die. We've little choice with what life gives us, no choice but to accept."

Kemu's tears welled up, and he sniffled, his voice choked with emotion. "Maybe it is better, maybe it's better to just die than to live in a prison," he said, his words heavy and burdened. "Yes, I'm weak, I've always been weak, and I know it. If I'm not designed for this world, maybe I'm better off on the other side."

"Don't say that Kemu," Chiri pleaded, his voice filled with gentle concern. "You're not weak, you're just hurting. You don't want me to leave, but you have just got to understand. Why do you want to make this so hard? Why do you think it would be the end of the world?"

"It would be," Kemu spoke fiercely, his gaze straight into Chiri's eyes. "It would be the end of the world. I love you, brother. I want you to be here with me, helping me as you've always done. With you gone, it would never be the same."

"I won't be gone forever, Kemu," Chiri now spoke with anger. "You are not a little kid anymore; you are a grown man. Act like an adult for once and know that you'll be the heir of this dynasty whether you like it or not."

Kemu then turned away, crying. This was the first time Chiri had raised his voice at him. Perhaps his brother was right, perhaps he was acting like a little child and needed to grow up.

Chiri realised that he had just shouted at his poor brother who was immensely troubled. He knew using anger would only make things worse, and he felt sorry for him. Chiri then stepped closer and wanted to place a comforting hand on Kemu's shoulder, but he shrugged him off.

"You should get going," Kemu said, his gaze fixed at the horizon, avoiding looking his brother in the eyes. "You wouldn't want to keep Charwe waiting. I wish you a safe journey."

Chiri didn't know what else to say to his brother. He felt sorry for him, for he knew that a storm was coming.

12

The City of Kings and Queens

"How far are we from the capital?" Hungwariri asked his chief, his voice tinged with exhaustion. They had been walking for days, and the weariness had begun to settle deep within his bones.

"Not far to go, we'll get there before sunset," Gwindi assured him.

Hungwariri looked around, at the towering trees above them. "I do not know much about this place," he told Chief Gwindi.

"This is Mthwakazi, young man, the territory of the amaNdebele. They are of the Nguni, a tribe of warriors," Chief Gwindi said. "The kingdom was established by Mzilikazi, after he had migrated from the south, when it was ripped apart by the Mfecane."

"What's that?" he asked.

"The crushing. The war in the southernmost part of this land that affected and destabilised the whole region, even this far north," Gwindi said. "It is said that thousands and thousands of people died during that time."

"I think we were quite fortunate to be born in times of peace," Hungwariri said. "I'm not sure I would want to survive in a time of war, having to worry about my family."

"Then you must be very much afraid," Gwindi said. "I fear that if the heavens are not in our favour, a second crushing might destroy us, maybe something worse than the Mfecane. We must be prepared for anything."

A chill swept through Hungwariri. He remembered the day he had quarrelled with his mother.

She had told him that it was not safe anymore, that he had to leave with his siblings.

She had obviously seen something, perhaps in her dreams. If only he had known then that his mother was someone powerful.

"Why do people even fight wars?" Hungwariri asked, now worried.

"Power gives pride, and every man craves for it. Pride elevates one's identity and firm place in history," Gwindi explained. "People with pride want others to bend to them, rather than them to others, so they find different ways to do that. What's more perfect than to weaken your opponent, then to take away all they possess and make it yours?"

"Why do they not think about the consequences of war and about the people that are killed?" the young boy asked.

"Because they don't care," Gwindi said. "There are men who fight for the people but there are those who fight for themselves, and those are the most dangerous."

"When war comes, I will fight for my people," Hungwariri spoke with unwavering conviction. "I'm a child, but I will stand to protect my own. I'm no coward."

"Quite a brave lad, aren't you!" Gwindi smiled at the boy. "My own heir would wish to be like you. If it ever comes to war, I'm sure Kemu would prefer to hide. Many people think he is a coward because he trembles in court, stammers when asked a question, and cries when he finds no answer. Well, I think that he is brave in his own way, maybe braver than his other brothers. Everyone else tries to hide their tears, and pretend to be brave, while in truth, no one really is."

Hungwariri smiled because he had heard many people say that Kemu was weak. Kemu was never made to sit on the Court, but he endured the pain anyway.

As they were walking, Gwindi stopped abruptly, and held Hungwariri back with his hand, "Wait, listen."

Hungwariri strained his ears, trying to discern any unusual sounds amidst the symphony of nature. And then he heard it, a distant rumble, faint but distinct. His eyes narrowed with concern, wondering what could have caused such a commotion in that forest.

Before he could voice his thoughts, the forest erupted with the deafening roar of gunfire. Panic gripped both Hungwariri and Gwindi as they realised, they were caught in the midst of a fire exchange.

Without hesitation, Gwindi yanked Hungwariri close and pulled him down, seeking refuge behind a thick bush. Their breaths came in rapid gasps as they watched the chaos unfold. Spear axes and assegais whizzed through the air, slicing through the once serene atmosphere.

Through the veil of leaves, Gwindi caught glimpses of Ndebele warriors, hiding behind trees. Gwindi couldn't understand. The Ndebele were already at war with the Europeans.

Hungwariri's eyes met those of a warrior hiding behind a nearby tree, and then realised that they recognised one another. The man was Takura, one of the boys from his village. He had been taken during the raids. He was now fighting as a warrior for Mthwakazi. In that fleeting moment that they recognised one another, an unspoken understanding passed between them.

With swift and silent movements, Takura beckoned his chief and Hungwariri to follow him. They crawled on their hands and knees, their bodies trembling with fear, and they could hear the shouts and cries of the combatants.

As they reached Takura's side, he motioned for them to stay low and led them deeper into the thicket.

Takura led them through a labyrinth of trees, their footsteps deft and sure, their senses heightened, attuned to every rustle and crackle in the undergrowth.

The cacophony of battle raged on, but it remained behind, as they started running through the trees. They did not stop running until they were sure they were out of danger.

Gwindi then looked up and realised he could see the thatched tops of the Ndebele Capital, KoBulawayo.

Takura then walked with Gwindi and Hungwariri into the clearing of the capital. This was their first time to walk into this grand capital of Mthwakazi. It was circled by dome shaped straw huts.

Women and children looked at Gwindi and Hungwariri with awe, as they approached the great Court of their king, the largest structure they had ever seen. It was guarded by warriors on either side, their hands tightly gripping long spears and large oval ox-hide shields.

These warriors were different from their own Zezuru warriors and were more organised. They wore a headdress and short cap made of black ostrich feathers, a kilt made of leopard skins and ornamented with the tails of white cattle. Around their arms they wore similar tails and around their ankles they wore rings of brass.

The colour of their shields varied from black, white, red or speckled, according to the regiment they belonged to.

Hungwariri could clearly see that this was the land of warriors, a territory of kings and queens.

Gwindi and Hungwariri ducked through the entrance and entered into the court where they found King Lobengula sitting regally on his throne next to his wife. His other wives, children and advisors were also there, sitting around him.

As the pair approached, Mlilo, the King's right-hand advisor, rose to his feet and his voice echoed in the hall as he addressed the two men approaching. "You stand in the presence of the King of Mthwakazi, Inkosi Yamabutho, Lobengula Khumalo, and his esteemed chief wife, Queen Lozikeyi Dlodlo."

Hungwariri stepped forward, his eyes fixed on the King. "Your Majesty, may I present Chief Gwindi of the Hwata dynasty."

"Welcome, Chief Gwindi," Mlilo spoke. "We are honoured by your presence. Pray tell, what brings you to our court?"

The Chief then stepped forward. "First of all, I need to know the reason for the crossfire that nearly took my life."

Mlilo turned to his king and translated Gwindi's words in their own Ndebele tongue. King Lobengula gave his reply, and then Mlilo translated it back to Gwindi. "If you were unaware, we are currently in an open war with the Europeans."

"Why are you at war with them?" Gwindi asked the King. "Yes, I understand that you are an ambitious clan, but they have stronger firearms, and you won't survive the war."

"We've not declared war, we are simply defending our territory, something you and your other chiefs have failed to do with yours," Mlilo translated his king's reply. "Right now, the Europeans are on the march towards this capital, and the fighters you saw out there are defending it with their lives."

"We've no need to defend our territories from the Europeans but your warriors," Gwindi said. "Our villages have long suffered from your raids, and we've had enough. Why are you taking our men and livestock?"

"The raids are necessary, I need more men to defend this capital and more livestock to feed them," Lobengula replied. "I've tried negotiating with some of your fellow chiefs, but it was to no avail. I had no time, and I had to use force."

"What you are implying here doesn't make any sense," he said. "The Europeans are simply traders. Why would they dare attack your capital? They have no right."

"It seems you've been fooled much like the rest of them. The Europeans are not traders but conquerors," Lobengula told him. "I am the only king left in this region. Once this capital falls, we will all be on our knees, and standing up again might be impossible."

"Well, what are the chances that you might be able to hold your capital?" Chief Gwindi asked, fear flowing in his veins.

"Last week we tried engaging them near Shangani River, but we were defeated, we lost one thousand five hundred men. Now my warriors are engaging the enemy at Bembesi, two thousand Matabele riflemen and four thousand warriors. If the odds are at our side, we will prevail."

"What if it goes otherwise?" Chief Gwindi asked. "What if they are defeated again?"

"We should not hope for that to happen," King Lobengula could only reply.

"But how did it ever go this bad?" Chief Gwindi shook his head in disbelief. "It almost seems like yesterday when the whole land had been in peace without any bloodshed."

"It's funny to think that it all started with three friends and a piece of paper. Who could ever know it would end up like this?" Lobengula spoke, grief in his voice. "Have you ever seen a chameleon catching a fly? The chameleon gets behind the fly and remains motionless for some time, then he advances very slowly and gently, first putting forward one leg and then the other. At last, when well within reach, he darts his tongue and the fly disappears. Europe is the chameleon, and I am that fly."

Chief Gwindi was troubled with all he had learned, and he feared for his own village. A storm was coming indeed.

13

The Thrashing

As soon as morning came, Kemu went to visit the spiritualist, Kapfumo. He found the man outside his hut, tending to his small garden.

Setting aside his hoe, Kapfumo turned to greet the Acting Chief with a warm smile. "Mangwanani, Kemu. What brings you here on this fine morning?"

Kemu's eyes darted nervously as he took a deep breath, gathering the courage to share his unsettling dream. "I had a restless night, Kapfumo," he confessed, his voice tinged with anxiety. "In my dream, I found myself walking along a narrow path, and suddenly, I witnessed a snake slithering across it. I've heard tales that such an encounter brings forth bad fortune, and it has left me fearful."

Kapfumo's eyes crinkled with understanding as he listened attentively to Kemu's words. Placing a reassuring hand on his shoulder, he spoke with a calm certainty. "Fear not, dear Kemu," his voice carried gentle reassurance. "While it is true that encountering a snake crossing your path in reality may signify misfortune, dreams are in a realm of their own. They often speak to us in symbols and metaphors, guiding us through the labyrinth of our subconscious minds. It might not necessarily mean bad fortune."

"I guess you are right," Kemu forced a smile, trying to feel hopeful. Kemu just wasn't feeling like himself. An odd feeling engulfed him. Then they heard distant hooves from the west, and when they turned, they saw some horses galloping towards their village. There were about five.

Kemuteku looked and then recognised the man that was riding in the front. It was Henry Pollard, their European friend that Chief Gwindi often invited to court.

The approaching horses caught the attention of the villagers who left their activities and gathered around to see who it was.

The horses then walked into the village and stood right at the centre. Pollard's face did not seem friendly, as it had usually been. The men that accompanied him were all armed with guns, and they did not have smiles on their faces.

He did not even care to look at the Hwata brothers and greet them as he usually did.

He cleared his throat and then spoke with great authority. "Listen up, everyone! I am glad to announce to you all that I'm your newly appointed Native Commissioner. I'll be supervising everything that's happening in this region and making sure that our government's laws are being strictly adhered to."

He spoke in their native tongue with his muddy accent, and it was quite hard for Kemu to make up some of his words.

"I'm sorry, but what government are you referring to?" Kapfumo stepped up, as he couldn't understand.

"Oh, you don't know?" he said. "Approximately forty kilometres away from here, we've developed our new capital, Fort Salisbury. This land is a British discovery and belongs to the Queen of England. You have a new government now, meaning new laws. With me, I have a list of all the duties that you must perform, and the taxes that you are expected to pay."

Henry started reading aloud the new laws and the villagers listened with a mix of confusion and concern. His unclear words echoed through the air, striking them all with a sense of dread.

The air grew heavy with tension, and whispers spread among the crowd. Some villagers exchanged worried glances, while others clenched their fists in frustration.

At that moment, Mutimumwe walked to Kemu and whispered to him. "Don't just stand there, idiot, do something!" Mutimumwe then pushed Kemu who stumbled forward, unable to stop his legs.

All eyes turned to him, their gazes filled with anticipation and uncertainty. Kemu's heart pounded hard against his chest, as a surge of panic engulfed him.

He didn't know what to do, and he knew that the villagers were expecting him to say or to do something. He then tried to regain himself and tried to act confident.

Chiri had told him to do something, to pretend to be brave. The world only sees the mask you wear and not the face beneath. He had to wear the mask of his position, a leader of all these people. He then summoned every ounce of courage he could muster.

Taking a deep breath, Kemu straightened his posture and raised his voice, his words trembling but determined. "You have no right!" he declared, his voice quivering yet filled with a newfound resolve. "This village is of the Hwata, and we accept no authority other than that of our chief."

Henry's eyes narrowed, a mix of surprise and admiration flickering across his face. He seemed intrigued by the young man's courage. He swiftly dismounted his horse and he approached the young boy, his boots crunching against the dusty ground.

The man, now standing face to face with Kemu, spoke softly, "I must compliment you. Your defiance is commendable. I like your spirit."

In a sudden and unexpected move, Henry delivered a sharp slap across Kemu's face. The sound echoed through the silence, leaving a print of Henry's hand on Kemu's face. Gasps of shock escaped the onlookers, their eyes widening in disbelief.

The other villagers tried to protest, but guns immediately pointed out to them.

The force of Henry's blow sent shockwaves through Kemu's entire being, causing his mouth to tremble uncontrollably. Tears welled up in his eyes, betraying the pain and humiliation he felt.

As Kemuteku struggled to hold back his tears, he glanced around at the villagers who looked at him, their eyes filled with a mix of sympathy and fear. He didn't want to cry in front of them, didn't want to show weakness, but the overwhelming emotions proved too much to bear. Silent tears streamed down his cheeks, their salty taste mingling with the bitter taste of abandonment.

"How dare you try to defy me?" Henry's voice boomed, laced with anger and authority. His piercing gaze bore into Kemu, who trembled under his intense scrutiny, his hand over his burning cheek.

Turning to his men, Henry issued a chilling command. "Tie this one to a tree. We have to teach him a little lesson, like what we did with Chief Chiweshe. He will be an example to everyone. No one must defy the Native Commissioner."

When he saw the men dismounting from their horses, Kemu's legs trembled and his heart raced as he pleaded for mercy, his voice quivering with fear. "Please, have mercy! I never meant any harm," he cried. His words were desperate and filled with regret. But Henry remained unmoved, his heart hardened.

Kemu fought against the iron grip of the two men, his muscles straining with every ounce of strength he could muster. But their hold was unyielding. His screams pierced the air, echoing through the village, a desperate plea for mercy.

"Please, don't!" a voice came from the crowd. "Forgive him. He is just young. He didn't know."

Kemu turned and saw that it was one of the men at court, Meda. He felt a bit of relief. He had walked up to save him when he thought no one would.

Meda wanted to walk closer to the native commissioner, but guns surrounded him.

"I recognise your authority as my native commissioner," he said. "Please, release Kemu and we will not oppose your authority."

"Begging for his release is just the same as opposing my authority," he told Meda. "You've angered me, surely. Now, his punishment will be more than the thrashing. After this, he will be tied to a horse and dragged through all his villages."

Meda dropped to his knees, tears threatening to spill from his eyes, begging. "Please, please don't."

Henry gave a wicked smile, as his men dragged Kemu closer to the tree. Kemu's mind raced, searching for a way to escape his impending fate. Kemu watched in horror when he saw the *sjambok* that Henry was handed. Henry grinned wickedly, flexing and stretching it to show Kemu how robust the rhinoceros hide was.

If only he had known, he could've run away, far where no one would see him. Kemu was weak, and weak people die. The storm had arrived to take him.

Meda could not do anything other than watch Kemu being thrashed. He swore that he was going to kill Pollard himself.

14

Fort Martin

Chinengundu Mashayamombe's village was situated beside some kopjes that were as massive as hills.

Charwe's arrival was warmly welcomed, and it had been greatly anticipated by Mashayamombe and his own spiritualist, Gumboreshumba.

The Chief and his spiritualist offered Charwe and Chiri a walk around his area, a beautiful landscape with kopje hills and vast herds of Buffalos and other wildlife.

"I hope your journey was pleasant, great Mhondoro. It's been long since I myself travelled a long distance," Chief Mashayamombe spoke as they walked. "Last time I travelled all the way to the east to visit the ruins of the old kingdom of Dzimbabwe. It's quite impressive, granite slabs sitting atop one another, to make very tall walls. It was simply magnificent to behold."

"I sometimes see glimpses of my past lives, in visions and dreams," Nehanda said, as they walked. "The old kingdom of Dzimbabwe was indeed a great one, and I wonder if it can ever be that great again."

"I heard from a tale that once in your past life, when you were Nyamhita, your father forced you to sleep with your brother," Gumboreshumba, the spiritualist said. "Have you also glimpsed that part of your past life?"

"We were not really forced," Nehanda said. "We both understood that we had to perform our duties. The Mutapa Empire was at the brink of falling, and the ritual was very necessary."

"How does it really work?" Chiri was curious to know. "I heard that in the old days, men would lie with other men or their sisters to increase power and wealth."

"I don't know, only that power is a mysterious thing that men crave," Nehanda said. "It can drive them to do absolutely anything to achieve it. The Kingdom of Dzimbabwe had crumbled, and my father had his hopes that he could restore its glory."

"And the ritual worked," Gumboreshumba said. "After Dzimbabwe had crumbled, Mutapa's kingdom was quite powerful. Nature and life walk in mysterious ways."

"Yes, it was powerful indeed," she replied. "But look, where is the empire now? Power makes us proud and boastful, but we forget that it destroys us. Men devote their lives to pursue more power, but the more they do, the more it corrupts them."

"Power isn't all bad,' Chiri said. "A powerful kingdom has happier and healthier people. There is less hunger and suffering. I think that power unites."

"Power requires blood. It was not only the *kupinga-pasi* ritual that increased the power of the Mutapa kingdom, but it was war and conquest. Blood must flow, that is why if someone tries acquiring power from a *sangoma*, a sacrifice must be made. Power unites people as much as it breaks them," Nehanda said.

"You are as clever as I thought you were. You really are her, the daughter of Murenga," the Chief said. "I was delighted when I heard that you were coming all this way to my humble village. I can only wonder, why has a great mhondoro like you travelled all the way?"

"There are certain rumours I've heard," Nehanda said. "I hear that you've bad blood with the traders and that you are planning to repel them. Why?"

"I see that rumours do travel really fast," Gumbo, the spiritualist, replied. "I'm certain you did not travel all this way just because of those rumours, but because of your instincts. Even though you don't know the reason, you can feel it, you can feel that they are dangerous and must be repelled."

Nehanda was now nervous, for what Gumboreshumba had just said was true. Her instincts were telling her that something was not right.

"They are traders who do not know their boundaries," the Chief explained his reasons. "They now claim our land for themselves. They own the gold in this land as much as we do. They now mine it on their own, for it is 'their land' after all. Recently, their police told us that my village was on their land, and we are tenants to them. We should pay or we get evicted. They call it the hut tax."

"Those who fail to pay will have to work for them, for free," Gumboreshumba added. "They are not the ones that are digging their gold, it's our villagers. They even told us that we cannot hunt for meat; they say that we are 'poaching' their wildlife. Our Chief is to report to them any developments, for they are more superior than he is."

The Chief then pointed out some farms on the other side of the valley. There were so many that they actually formed a village of their own. "They are now building their homes here, as it is their land after all. They do not care to consult me unless they want their tax."

"Well, has there been anything done about this?" Chiri asked. "What you are saying here is quite absurd.

"Actually, we are laying out plans to attack that settlement in the night," Chief Mashayamombe said. "We are gathering the men and making the arrows and spears for them to use. We have a few rifles; they will help us. We will start by killing the man that calls himself the Native Commissioner of this village, David Mooney."

"It's going to be hard though, because of some chiefs," Gumboreshumba said. "Many are ignorant. Many are being bribed. Many like the idea of having a foreign entity to govern them. It's all just chaos. A few have pledged in their arms to join in the effort, the likes of Chikwakwa, Seke, Kunzwi and Mangwende."

"So the traders are the enemy," Nehanda could now confirm all that had been troubling her. "I had seen them before; I had been forewarned in a dream. At first, I couldn't understand, but now…"

"The kneeless men?" Gumboreshumba asked, then smiled at her when he realised that she was shocked with how he knew about them. "I saw them in a dream too, a vision shown to me by Murenga. We share the same gift, dear sister."

Nehanda could not understand, so he went on to explain it to her.

"I am Kaguvi, son of Murenga Pfumojena Sororenzou," Gumbo told her. "I am here for the same reason that you are here. To resist this creature that has entered our lands."

"Kaguvi Gumboreshumba has already been able to convince other chiefs to start this uprising and restore our lands to their former selves, and so must you." Mashayamombe spoke. "We've welcomed crows into this land, and now it is time to chase them away. We ask you to join us as we begin to fight them off."

"We shall return home at once and gather up men to also repel them," Charwe said. "We thank you for shedding on us the light we needed. A storm is truly coming."

"No," Kaguvi Gumboreshumba said. "It's not coming, it has already arrived. As you said, power requires blood. The kneeless are in our land to pursue power, and I can smell the blood that is going to flow. Lots of it!"

15

The Fall of KoBulawayo

Before Gwindi could depart KoBulawayo, one of the King's court officials, Mukwati, visited him in the hut that he had been staying in.

"Goredema Gwindi, descendent of the three Hwata conquerors," Mukwati said as he walked into the hut. "I've heard many stories about how your dynasty came to be. Three brothers who fled their villages, then started a whole dynasty from nothing. They were very ambitious men."

"It was not only about ambition," Gwindi said. "They wanted to change the current, to change the divided Zezuru and unite them under one kingdom just as it had been centuries ago."

"One can never go against the current, or they'll only crash," the man said. "Conquerors are not always heroes.

Shayachimwe and his brothers will always be villains to the people they conquered."

"Shayachimwe will always be a hero," Goredema told him. "He made the lives of the people better than they were. He changed the region and formed a greater dynasty from it."

"Did he?" The man asked. "Who had told him that the people never enjoyed the lives that they were living, that they needed a saviour to kill their rulers and conquer them? Did he really do it for their sake, or for his own sake, and his own power, and own legacy?"

"What would you prefer? A divided Zezuru, or one strong nation, under one strong ruler?" Gwindi asked him.

"As I told you, one can never go against the current," the man explained. "The division of the kingdom was already prophesied a long time ago, along with this war. There's nothing else we can do about prophecy than to just watch it unfold."

"And what do you know about prophecy?" Gwindi asked.

"More than you do, dear Gwindi," Mukwati said. "Just like your new spiritualist, Charwe Nyakasikana, I'm a Mhondoro, guardian spirit of this land. We've all returned for one last time, to watch the unfolding of a prophecy and the breaking of culture."

"No, that's not true," Gwindi said. "You have not returned to watch our fall, but to save us from it."

"I'm afraid this is the beginning of the end," Mukwati said. "We might fight and win, but an even greater trouble shall come after this one. Men shall arise and claim to stop the storm but shall be the storm themselves. A dark spirit is upon us, dear Gwindi. Even us, the Mhondoro, cannot stop it."

"We cannot let a storm decimate us. Let's use Shayachimwe's idea for our two territories. This will end when we've united the Zezuru and the Ndebele, you and the other Mhondoro. We will drive the Europeans away and stop the storm once and for all."

"The storm is not only the Europeans," Mukwati said. "We are destroying one another. We are our own pain and downfall. This war was started by impis who betrayed our king and whispered lies to him. Even if we chase away the Europeans, everything else is all rot."

Before Gwindi could speak, they heard loud shouts coming from outside. "The defence line has been breached! The defence line has been breached! Take your things and depart the capital! The defence line has been breached!"

Gwindi turned to Mukwati with confusion. "What's going on out there?"

"Men shall be blown away as easily as chaff in the rain. The storm has arrived on the shores of KoBulawayo," Mukwati spoke with sadness in him. "We must burn everything now before they capture it, as per Nguni tradition."

"But what would be the fate of the King of the amaNdebele?" Gwindi panicked.

"He will leave the capital and go somewhere else where he is safe," Mukwati told him. "I will remain behind with his queen, Lozikeyi, and surrender the capital for a little while and strategise a second Matabele war."

Gwindi then walked outside the hut where Hungwariri had been waiting for him. There was panic all over the capital and everyone was running around, taking their livestock and children. Flames blazed in the night, as people burned down their homes.

"We have to leave now before they come!" Hungwariri was terrified. Hungwariri and Gwindi started running.

A sudden and thunderous roar then erupted, and everyone lowered down. The night was as bright as day.

The deafening sound of the explosion reverberated through the air, causing everyone to instinctively drop to the ground for cover. Gwindi and Hungwariri turned and saw flames soaring into the night sky, painting it in shades of orange and red.

Everyone thought the Europeans had started their assault on the village, but it had only been the amaNdebele ammunition magazine that had exploded because of the fire.

The screaming intensified and everyone ran for safety. Gwindi and Hungwariri also ran towards the forest, so that they could escape the war and return to their village.

They did not stop running, and the chaos seemed to follow them. In the forest, the screams had been replaced with gunshots. The European troops were now closing in.

Gwindi and Hungwariri just ran wherever their feet took them, not knowing if they were running towards the troops or away from them. The sounds of gunshots seemed to be coming from everywhere in that dark forest.

Suddenly, a searing pain ripped through Gwindi's side, and he stumbled, collapsing to the ground. Hungwariri turned, his eyes widening in terror as he witnessed his Chief's fall.

"Chief!" the boy cried, his voice choked with anguish. Hungwariri knelt beside his Chief, who now had blood flowing in gushes from his chest. The young boy did not know what to do.

Gwindi was in great pain, but he was determined to find the strength to speak to the young boy. "Go now, young boy, go and find our village, go and warn them all."

Tears mingled with the dirt on Hungwariri's cheeks as he clutched Gwindi's hand refusing to let go. "No, I can't leave you here. We've got to go together. You are their chief; they are waiting for you."

"Go now child," the chief whispered, his voice trembling. "Run and tell them to fight without me." With a trembling nod, Hungwariri reluctantly released his chief's hand and rose to his feet.

The gunshots were still being fired. As the boy sprinted through the dense foliage, his heart weighed heavy with grief and fear. The forest seemed to stretch on endlessly, its shadows whispering secrets of danger and uncertainty. He kept on running until the sounds of the gunshots became distant and ended up fading in the background.

He was running to warn them all, he was running to tell them that they were in the midst of a raging storm.

16

The Sting

Nehanda and Chiri had spent most of the day walking, and finally, they reached their village just as the sun was setting. The villagers, noticing their arrival, gathered around, their eyes etched with worry. Both Nehanda and Chiri could feel the sense of unease hanging in the air.

Kapfumo walked forward to greet Nehanda Charwe and Chiri, sharing the same sadness that had been on everyone's faces.

"Is everything ok?" Chiri quickly asked.

"No, nothing is ok. Something happened when you were gone," Kapfumo spoke, with heavy sadness on him. "Kemu is being tended to in the healer's hut."

"The healer's hut, what happened to him?" Chiri asked with worry.

When Kapfumo took too long before speaking, Chiri knew that something was wrong. Without wasting another moment, he sprinted towards the healer's hut, his legs carrying him as fast as the beating heart within him.

As he burst through the entrance of the hut, his eyes fell upon a scene that sent a shiver down his spine. There, lying on a mat, Kemu seemed barely alive. His eyes were closed, and his breathing was shallow. Chiri felt a surge of pain and fear. He knelt by his brother's side and took his hand.

Nehanda walked in and saw Meda standing in the hut.

"What happened?" She asked him, seeing her brother lying there, his body covered in fresh scars.

"The Native Commissioner thrashed the boy, and then dragged him on the ground with a horse."

"What the heck is a Native Commissioner? Kemuteku is the heir of this dynasty, the one who sits at the Chief's place. Whatever offence he committed, this should not be done to him, it is treason," Chiri said, his eyes red with tears and fury.

Chiri then noticed that Kemuteku opened his eyes slowly, and Chiri had a spark of hope within him. "Kemu, Kemu, can you hear me?"

Kemuteku looked at Chiri with a faint smile. His brother had finally arrived, the one he had wanted to see all along. "Chiri…you came…"

"I'm here, by your side, as I promised." Chiri felt tears sting his eyes. He tried to sound hopeful. "Kemu, you're going to be fine. You'll be back to your old self, and then we'll go out there and show them all who the Hwata brothers are."

Kemu shook his head weakly. "No, Chiri…I won't…it's too painful. I feel pain everywhere, it's hurting, Chiri. The horse, I wanted the horse to stop but it was running fast. I can feel it. I'm dying, and I want to."

Chiri gasped. He refused to believe it. "No, no, no, Kemu. Don't say that. You're the strongest person I know. You are my brave eland bull, Museyamwa."

Kemu sighed. "Chiri, I'm weak, you know, I've always been. I was weak when he came to me with a sjambok. I let them hurt me. I let them hurt our people. I allowed them to take everything, now they are taking me away from you. I'm weak, and weak people die."

Chiri shook his head. "No, Kemu. You're not weak, and they are not taking you away. Don't allow them."

Kemuteku smiled sadly. "I told him… that snake in my dream, it meant something. Chiri, you told me that I was going to be a good ruler, but I failed."

"You're our brave Hwata Prince, you've always been. I will never ever leave your side again," Chiri promised.

"Chiri…you're too kind to me. You always were. But you don't have to lie to me now. I know the truth. I know I failed you. I failed our father. I failed our dynasty. I could've pretended to be strong for you, but I'm not even good at pretending," Kemuteku closed his eyes, as tears trickled from them. "The wounds are too painful, Chiri. I can't handle them anymore, I just can't. I wish I'd just died when the horse was still pulling me. I've tried sleeping, but I can't. I just want to sleep forever, to sleep and never wake again. I want to go, Chiri."

Chiri clenched his teeth as he shook his head. "No, you are not going anywhere. I'm demanding you to stay with me. This is an order. Pain never lasts, wounds always heal."

Kemu squeezed Chiri's hand, and then spoke with difficulty. "Keep on being my strong brother and show wrath to all of them. Avenge my death. Show them who you are, promise me that." Chiri nodded, and then Kemuteku smiled.

Chiri then looked up at Nehanda, "He is dying, can't you do something?"

She stood there and watched Chiri crying for his brother. She hated herself for it. She felt a pang of sorrow and guilt.

They called her Nehanda, they called her the most powerful spirit medium ever, yet she couldn't help him. She didn't know how to help him. Chiri then held his brother's hand in his arms and started singing a song for him. Finally, after a while, Kemuteku closed his eyes, and then exhaled softly. Chiri noticed it, then shook him a little bit, calling him to see any response. The healer walked to Kemu, and then confirmed that the young Chief was truly gone.

Chiri screamed. He hugged Kemu's cold body and cried. Nehanda also wept, as she watched her two brothers, one dead, the other, broken.

"I watched him being whipped. I listened to his screams," Meda said, watching Chiri crying. "That native commissioner is a cruel man. I swear by the sacred pool named Peace; I will kill him myself."

Chiri cried throughout the night. He cried until he had no tears left, until he could feel a pain in his throat. Nehanda and Meda stood watch the whole night.

The villagers outside started wailing and singing, bidding farewell to their young Hwata Prince.

Their singing danced in Nehanda's ears, alongside Chiri's wails. She hated seeing him in pain, and she knew that there was only one way to answer to this madness by the invaders. They had to face the raging storm.

17

The Coronation

All the Hwata Villagers had gathered atop Shavarudzi hill underneath the moonlight, sadness shrouding their faces.

Chiri looked at Kemuteku's fresh grave, sitting amongst the graves of their other great ancestors. His brother had still been young, and never got the chance to feel the world around him. The man that took his life had not even thought about that, and about how he was important to all of them. Chiri was as angry as he was sad.

The sombre atmosphere hung heavy in the air, as silence enveloped the gathering.

As the crowd stood united in sorrow, their attention shifted to Hungwariri, who arrived at the shrine, breathless and panting.

Charwe's face brightened a bit, to the sight of her son. She had missed his face.

With determined steps, Hungwariri made his way towards his mother, and his older father, Chiri, who stood side by side, their faces etched with sorrow. Falling to his knees before Chiripanyanga, Hungwariri struggled to catch his breath before delivering his urgent message.

"We fled from the ravages of war in the south," he gasped, his voice trembling with a mix of fear and urgency. "But tragedy befell us. The Chief... he was shot before we could escape far. He told me to warn you all, war is coming for our villages. They are coming and they will destroy everything."

Hungwariri's words hung in the air, piercing through the sombre atmosphere. The news of impending danger cast a dark shadow over the already heavy hearts of those gathered. The funeral had transformed into a moment of reckoning, as the weight of the future pressed upon them all.

Charwe had a heavy sadness on her, and she turned to Chiri who had been holding back his screams. "Chief Gwindi is dead, along with his heir. You must take up his place and prepare us to face this storm that is looming. You must lead us into war, dear brother."

Chiri could hardly keep his breath. He had never thought he could ever feel so overwhelmed and conflicted. He found himself not wanting, just like Charwe never wanted to be a medium, just like Kemu never wanted to face the consequences of being a leader. He didn't want to but there was no one else who could do it, if not him.

Chiri looked up and then he saw the people assembling around him, eagerly awaiting for his response. He looked out at the multitude of expectant faces. The thought of leading his people in a time of war filled him with an overwhelming mix of fear and determination.

He gazed up at the night sky, at the twinkling stars above, as if to seek assurance from them. Tears welled up in his eyes as he gave a nod, accepting the position.

Chiri then went on his knees, and five mbira players surrounded him, playing a soft soothing melody, as Nehanda retrieved the royal spear axe from where it laid, next to Kemu's grave. Chiri closed his eyes, allowing the mbira melody to wash over him and to calm his heart, grounding him in that moment.

Nehanda walked towards Chiri with two men holding fire torches beside her. The flickering torches cast dancing shadows upon her face as she raised her voice, "Chiripanyanga, son of Guvamombe and grandson of Shayachimwe. I proclaim you Chief Hwata and the great Seyamwa of our dynasty. I proclaim this with the authority of all our ancestors, of all the Mhondoro, of Murenga the great, and of the creator, Musikavanhu himself."

Nehanda then reached up to where Chiri was kneeling and handed him the spear axe.

Chief Hwata Chiripanyanga then rose up in unison with the applause and ullulations from the crowds.

Tears streamed down his eyes, as he looked at all the people who ululated and cheered for him, at all those people who were depending on him to save them from the storm that had already entered their land. Even the singing birds in the trees seemed to have been praising him as well.

The wind seemed to talk to him for the very first time, telling him to raise his head up high, telling him that everything was on his shoulders now. The stars in the sky seemed to remind him to burn his flame though the darkness that had shrouded his people, to shine the whole Hwata dynasty with his light. The trees were reminding him to stand up like the eland that he was, to stand tall and to fight for what he knew was his.

Chiri was now the Chief, and he knew he had to act like one. He wiped his tears and blinked back those that threatened to spill from his eyes. He took a deep breath and faced his people with a straightened posture.

It was hard to keep his head up high, but he kept it that way.

"Now, Chief Hwata," Kapfumo started. "How do you suggest we respond to the murder of our chief and his heir by these invaders?"

Chiri himself wasn't sure if he was ready for that conversation yet. He then turned to Charwe, who gave him a reassuring nod. He took a breath before he turned back to answer the question.

"I'm afraid war is the only way to fight this parasite before it sucks us dry. We cannot negotiate with the kneeless. They own nothing here, not even a grain of sand. They came from another land, and they must return and leave us be."

"We cannot," Mutimumwe stepped in, "Everything belongs to them now, including us all."

"Why should we allow strangers to take what is ours?" Nehanda asked. "We must fight for it and must never tire. They are the ones that declared the war first by killing our chief and taking our gold and our land. We must avenge his death."

"Declaring war with them is no different to marching straight to our graves," Mutimumwe said. "If the amaNdebele capital itself is being crushed, who are we to stand against them? They are literally more powerful. They are gods. They are more advanced than us in every possible way. We should just surrender. They have absolutely everything."

"If they had everything, they would've no need to come from their faraway lands and invade our own," Chiri said. "They are here because we have what they do not have. They are here to steal everything we have, and we cannot allow them."

"They have firearms. If you have never seen them, I have," Mutimumwe said. "They are faster than your arrows, and they have a sound louder than the thunder you hear during a storm. Our spear axes will be no match."

"I've seen firearms before, Mutimumwe," Chiri said. "The dynasty has been trading with the Portuguese. There are a few, but we also have them. We can use them to our advantage."

"Do we even have men who know how to use them?" Kapfumo asked sceptically. He had never held a gun in his life, and he doubted that many of his fellow warriors had either.

Chiri turned towards the crowds, hoping to find a handful of people that might know how to use a firearm.

Chiri raised his voice and asked, "Is there anyone here who knows how to use firearms? Anyone with an idea of how they work?"

The silence was deafening. No one stepped forward. No one raised their hand. Chiri felt a pang of disappointment and frustration.

He was about to give up and move on, when he heard a voice from the back of the crowd, "I can." A young and thin man then walked forward, pushing his way through the people. He reached the front of the crowd and stood before Chiri.

"I'm Masvi, son of Gotora," he said. "When the white men came to my village, they took all the boys including me. They trained me to use the guns, and made me a police officer, and I served as a black watcher. When I got the chance, I deserted the camp. I can help some of the men to use the gun, using the knowledge I gained."

Hwata studied Masvi for a few seconds, then nodded slightly.

"Well then," Chief Hwata spoke to the young man. "You will be our firearm instructor and second commander of the army, and you must train these men to your best capabilities."

Masvi swallowed hard and bowed his head. "Thank you, sir," he said. "I will do my best."

Chiri nodded again and turned to address the crowd. "Now we need warriors! Men who are willing to die for the freedom of their people. Men who are willing to take their spear axes and arrows to fight for what's theirs."

There was a moment of silence, as everyone looked around nervously. Some shook their heads; others shrugged their shoulders. They were afraid.

Nehanda could also see this, and she stepped forward.

"If you bear the hearts and wear the faces of warriors, their weapons shall turn into water before your eyes," Nehanda proclaimed to them. "But if you cower and flee, their weapons shall pierce your backs and your souls. We have to drive them from our land. They are the ones bringing trouble upon us. They are the ones responsible for the drought, locust plagues and the rinderpest ravaging our cattle. We need to drive them back if we wish everything to return back to how it was."

"If you feel compelled to fight for your land, please walk forward," Chief Hwata commanded. "If you wish to die a hero, rather than a coward. If you understand that we are kings in our land, and not servants, walk forward. If you believe you are a true descendant of Murenga, please walk forward."

The Chief swept his gaze over the crowd, looking for a spark of courage. Slowly, one by one, some of the people picked up spear axes, and raised them, shouting their allegiance. Others followed suit, until a roar of defiance filled the air. They all rose up to sing a war song, a new energy flowing within them.

Mutimumwe looked around to see every man raising a spear axe and singing along to the war songs. He couldn't fathom how they had all fallen for this reckless idea of waging a war. He thought they must all be insane. He felt a surge of fear and disgust. He was not a coward, but he was not a fool either. He knew better. Mutimumwe then quietly slipped away from the crowd and disappeared in the shadows.

18

The war council

The flickering flames of torches cast eerie shadows on the rugged walls, as the war Council convened deep within the heart of Shavarudzi cave.

"I bring urgent news from Mukwati in the south," Kapfumo began, capturing the attention of the Council. "Queen Lozikeyi Dlodlo, aided by her twin brother, Muntuwani, now commands the royal army and leads a formidable second wave of the amaNdebele resistance."

The Council members exchanged glances, their expressions a mixture of determination and concern.

"We have also been informed of other Zezuru chiefs who have already launched their attacks, such as Chikwaka and Mugwedi," Chiri revealed. "Now, it is time for us to join forces and strike back."

Charwe gazed at her son, Hungwariri. His presence at the Council bothered her. He was just a child, yet he was standing amongst all the other grownups planning a war.

"How many fighters do we have?" Kapfumo asked.

"From all villages, we've managed to gather two thousand," Chiri said. "Twenty men have shown quite considerable skill in using the guns under the training of Masvi. They will be at the frontline of the war."

"There are still too few to win a war, but we can still win it with the right strategy," Masvi said. "We've increased the number of spears, bows and arrows, and new ones are being made as we speak now. Our enemies have more guns, and we cannot attack them head on with our spear axes. If it ever comes to an open field battle, we first use arrows, and when we push in close, we then use the spear axes."

"This will not be an open field battle," Chiri said. "We do not intend to massacre them, but to drive them away, so they know that we are resisting their occupation."

"We are at war, and war is about killing and dying," Hungwariri spoke up. "Spare them, and they'll stab us in the back. We must show them the consequences of their intrusion. We must eliminate every last one of them."

A murmur of agreement rippled through the Council, as some warriors nodded in support of Hungwariri's words. Nehanda was not agreeing with them, not because the words were wrong, but because Hungwariri was not supposed to be the one telling them.

"Hungwa is right," Masvi said. "If we want to win this war, we must not think of mercy, but we have to be ruthless. There is no time to act good and to feel sympathy, and our enemies know that."

"We will only kill those who attack us, or those who resist us," Chiri said firmly. "We must not forget who we are and where we come from. There are ways expected of a true warrior."

"We must chase them all away, but one must remain." Hungwariri said. "Kemu's blood yearns for vengeance. The commissioner stays at a police station, a distance from the settlement. He should be captured."

"Hungwariri," Charwe looked into her son's eyes. "You are still not of age. It is best for you to just observe, and to listen. That's how you learn."

"No mother, I want to fight too," he said. "I will learn to use the rifle under the training of Masvi, and fight to protect you, and Svotwa and Tandi. Hwata is my territory too, and if it means that I will die for it, I will gladly do it."

"No, you won't," Chiri told the boy.

Chiri could clearly see that Charwe was never going to fully convince Hungwariri to not fight in the war.

Hungwariri tried to protest, but Chiri raised his hand. "By the order of your chief, you will not be involved in the war. You are not of age, young boy."

Hungwariri was quick to anger. Without further protest, he stormed out of the cave with anger. Charwe looked at Chiri, and nodded a thank you to him.

"Quite a loss," Masvi said. "That boy could've been quite of help."

"He is young," Meda spoke. Nehanda could swear this was the first time he ever spoke at court. "He needs time to learn, though what he suggested is actually right. I was there when Kemu was thrashed. The commissioner took away Kemu from us. The only price for treason is death, I'm sure we are all familiar with that law."

A murmur of agreement rose from the gathered, and Chiri made his final decision.

"Masvi, you will lead the attack on the settlements, using as minimum aggression as possible," he said. "I will go with Meda and five other troops and infiltrate the station to capture the Commissioner myself. I will make sure that he is brought to court alive."

Masvi laughed for a little bit, and everyone was silent to know why he had been laughing. "What do you mean by 'minimum aggression'? A war is not about using your feelings, but your weapons and the whole of your strength. We are all grown up men and no one here can fathom the consequences of this plan of yours."

"Can you please be direct with what you want to say," Chiri looked at Masvi.

"You are planning on attacking a settlement, and chase them away like you are chasing some chicken, and abduct one of their leaders, and execute him, then you expect the war to end as simple as that?"

"If they try to attack us again, we will just repel them," Chiri said.

"You shouldn't say 'if' They will definitely attack, and they will demand blood, not the mercy that you offer them," Masvi said. "They are not chickens, they are conquerors, and they are more powerful than you think."

"Note that you are speaking to your chief, young man," Kapfumo warned him. "Standing in his Council does not make you his equal."

"I did not say I'm his equal, I'm only spitting facts," Masvi said. "Is it not the reason why we are all gathered here, to make out a plan?"

"Which is what we've just done," Chiri said. "You are just trying to complicate things. We've said that we will chase them away, and if they ever return to attack us, we have a front line of your men, then we have spear axes and arrows. We fight them."

"Ok then," Masvi said. "I've understood your plan, and it is to send all the Hwata men to their graves. In Matebeleland, they used what they call the maxim guns. I've seen one, and you haven't. When the day comes, you'll see what maxim guns can do, and I hope you will live another day to tell other people of what they can do."

Masvi then bowed before his chief and left the room, even though he had not been dismissed.

19

The Attack

Under the cover of darkness, Chiri's group stealthily made their way through overgrown fields, their rifles held tightly in their hands. Their movements were swift and silent, shadows blending with shadows as they crept closer. Their mission was simple: infiltrate the station and capture the man they wanted, Henry Hawkins Pollard. They wanted him, dead or alive. As they approached the farmstead, their hearts raced with anticipation.

Meanwhile, less than a league away, Masvi led his warrior troops towards the settlement.

Even after Masvi had pleaded for him to reconsider his plans, Chiri had not changed them. He was going to do just as they had discussed in the war Council.

Meda was by Chiri's side, slowly creeping towards the small police station, situated between some hills.

To their surprise, the entire place appeared deserted, as if the inhabitants had been forewarned of their arrival and fled. Chiri and Meda exchanged confused glances, their eyes scanning the empty station and abandoned fields. It was an eerie sight, the silence broken only by the rustling of leaves in the wind.

However, they continued moving their way towards the station. The wooden planks creaked under their weight, adding an unsettling sound to their stealthy advance. Their senses were heightened, every nerve on edge, as they listened for any sign of life.

Just as they reached the back of the house, a faint sound caught their attention. It was the unmistakable clip-clop of hooves on the road. Chiri and Meda exchanged a quick glance, their eyes filled with determination. They knew they had to find out what it was.

They moved swiftly, staying low to avoid being seen, until they reached a vantage point where they could see the cart driving off in the distance. The cart was being driven with a sense of urgency, and it was clear that the people inside were trying to escape.

Chiri, his voice barely above a whisper, said, "They are using the road, we can catch up with them if we go using the other side of the hill."

Meda nodded, and then turned to motion for their other troops to follow behind them.

As Chiri and Meda hurriedly made their way around the hill, the other soldiers followed closely behind, their hearts pounding. The setting sun cast long shadows across the landscape, adding an eerie atmosphere to the scene. They reached the designated spot and took cover behind a cluster of boulders, and they now could see the cart, a bit closer than it had been.

"Keep your arrows ready," Meda whispered to the soldiers they had, his voice barely audible over the rustling leaves. "Shoot only when your target is in view, we do not want to waste our arrows."

The soldiers nodded, their expressions a mix of determination and nervousness. Moments later, the distant clip-clop of hooves reached their ears, growing louder with each passing second. The horse cart came into view, its wooden wheels creaking under the weight of its cargo.

The cart carried Henry and five other European police men. The other native officers were all notably missing from the cart. They had been informed about the ambush beforehand, and had already fled, without even informing their other workmates.

Henry and his men only knew about the ambush much later, and they were hoping that it wasn't too late. One of the police in the cart, Blakistone, was shaking, and it was as if the rifle he was holding was going to fall. He had to stay alert as they had been expecting an attack anytime.

Blakiston was barely a man, and his heart was pounding quite hard, he could hear it in his ears. His eyes gazed everywhere, his ears listening to any rustle, afraid that something might appear from the grass. The horses weren't moving as fast as he wanted them to.

Suddenly, as he had anticipated, a spear flew and stabbed one of his fellow officers, Cass. He was the first to fall. Before they could figure out where the assault was coming from, another arrow flew and Dickinson met a similar fate as his fellow, Cass.

"Stay low! They are hiding in the bush!" The Native Commissioner informed Blakiston and two other remaining officers.

Arrows whizzed through the air, and the third body crumpled to the ground. Now only one other officer remained in the cart, and arrows continued and came from all angles.

One of their horses then neighed and suddenly stumbled as a arrow found its mark. The carriage crashed down, tossing all of them to the ground. The other officer was crushed under it and blood splashed.

Blakiston gave out an unmanly scream as he saw the blood, but Henry told him they had no time for all of that, and he stood up so they could quickly escape.

Blakiston got up and started running with Henry but realised that Henry was struggling to keep up. He saw that the Commissioner was wounded, and that there was a trail of blood behind him.

Blakiston urged Henry to run, pushing through the thick underbrush. Henry's injured leg slowed them down, and the native soldiers closed in, their capture imminent. Blakiston's fear left him no choice but to leave Henry. He started running and quickly found cover behind a sturdy tree, his heart pounding in his chest.

The sounds of Henry's anguished cries pierced the air as the soldiers closed in on him. Blakiston could hear Henry screaming curses as the soldiers captured him.

Blakiston waited until all the screaming and gunshots ceased. He then cautiously peered out from his hiding spot, hoping against hope that he had escaped unnoticed. To his dismay, he spotted one native man gesturing towards him, an arrow trained on his trembling form.

Blakiston quickly raised his arms, to show the man that he was now unarmed.

"Mercy," he cried. "Please, don't kill me."

Chiri kept pointing his spear at the young officer and couldn't understand what he was saying in his own strange, foreign tongue.

Chiri had wanted to release his arrow but then his eyes softened as he took in Blakiston's obvious fear. That would surely be the same way Kemu would have trembled if an arrow had been pointed at him.

Henry had been caught, and their mission was accomplished. Killing this trembling man was now pointless, so Chiri took a deep breath and signalled for Blakiston to flee, sparing his life.

Chiri watched, as the officer ran away in the wild for his dear life. Chiri then turned and walked to his other soldiers.

"We've got the Native Commissioner, we have to go with him to the village," Masvi said. "He has to be tried and executed today."

One warrior then arrived where they had been to deliver a message. "Meda and the others were able to chase away the settlers, but we've suffered many losses."

Masvi then looked right at Chiri, as if he wanted to tell him 'I told you so.'

20

The Hand of Justice

Nehanda Charwe knew that Chiri could not handle passing on the judgement, and she knew she had to do it for him.

Nehanda summoned the Commissioner, her voice echoing with authority. The man was brought before her, his hands bound tightly with coarse ropes. Dragged to his knees, he presented a pitiful sight, his face smeared with blood from the merciless beating he had endured at the hands of his captors.

She then saw Meda moving forward, a blade under his grip. He made an oath, swore on the sacred pool named Peace, that he was going to kill the commissioner himself.

Nehanda then turned to the accused. "You have taken the life of an heir to our dynasty," she declared, her voice resonating with a mix of grief and righteous anger. "Your act demands justice, for it strikes at the very heart of our Hwata dynasty. We must show the world that we honour and protect our leaders, and that such actions will not go unpunished."

The commissioner spat on her face and cursed in his own tongue, "Go to hell!"

Undeterred by the commissioner's disrespectful act, Nehanda wiped the spittle from her face, her resolve only growing stronger. She continued, her voice steady and commanding, "I, Nehanda Nyakasikana, the great Mhondoro of this land, sentence you to your death."

Meda swiftly moved behind the man, then held his chin, lifted his head up then slashed his throat. Meda kept on lifting the chin, as blood spurted out, painting a vivid image of justice being served. The onlookers watched in awe and horror as Henry Hawkins Pollard struggled in pain, his life slowly seeping away.

When the commissioner's body went still, Meda released his grip on the chin, and the lifeless body dropped down on the ground. Nehanda turned away, her duty fulfilled.

"Take this man," Nehanda commanded, "Throw his body into the river, so that it does not stink."

Chiri watched in silence, his eyes fixed on the lifeless form being dragged away. His mouth tightly clenched, he felt a mix of emotions all at once. It was justice for his brother, he thought, but the weight of the moment was heavy on his shoulders.

It was all in his mind as he made his way back to his hut, his steps slow and heavy. He thought he would find comfort in his familiar hut, but he failed to find it.

He laid down on his mat and longed for a good sleep, something that could help him escape all the turmoil troubling him.

Restlessly, Chiri tossed and turned, his mind unwilling to find peace. He could almost hear the soft whispers of the wind outside, carrying memories of Kemu's laughter and the weight of unspoken words. All he could see was blood, and screams. Unable to bear the thoughts any longer, he rose from his mat and made his way outside.

Underneath the moonlit sky, Chiri found himself walking toward the cliff where Kemu used to seek solace. As he sat on the edge, the cool night air caressed his face, and the distant sound of flowing water filled his ears. The moon cast a gentle glow upon the landscape.

Fear gripped Chiri's heart, intertwining with the anger and grief that consumed him. He felt afraid of everything now — the world seemed vast and unpredictable.

He remembered the last night that he had been sitting with Kemu on that cliff, now a distant sweet memory. Looking at the vast and beautiful hills, Chiri realised the reason why Kemu would always sit on that cliff. The landscape looked magical and offered a sense of escape.

He wondered if Kemu had finally found that place of his dream, the forest with blooming flowers of every colour, filled with animals running free. Some place where he would always smile and never cry. He felt a longing to be in such a forest, running and laughing with his brother.

When he tried to picture it in his mind, he found tears flowing down his cheeks, uncontrollably. He was not a boy who used to cry often. He actually tried to think if he had ever cried before the death of his brother.

"What are you doing out here, in this cold," he heard Charwe's voice, then turned to her as she sat beside him. "What are you thinking about?"

Chiri couldn't find the strength to reply. Instead, he gazed up at the moon, as if he was trying to read something written upon it.

Charwe also turned to the moon, understanding that it had all been a bit too much for her brother.

"I heard a tale," Charwe said, looking up at the moon that shone down on their faces. "About a Rozvi king who wanted his men to take down the moon, so he could use it as a plate."

"Quite an ambitious pursuit," Chiri smiled a bit, the memories of the tale coming back to him. "Thousands of people died, trying to build a staircase that could reach the moon. That's a sad tale, perhaps quite as sad as our own tale."

"I don't think that ours is a sad tale," Charwe turned to him. "It might be impossible to reach for the moon, but it's possible to fight for our freedom."

"Masvi was right," Chiri spoke with sadness. "This is just the beginning. We've poked a stick in a bees nest. We've started something we might not be able to stop. They are coming, and they will end us all."

"If they don't stop, we won't stop too," Charwe told her chief. "We will stand strong like we did today, stand up like the true descendants of Murenga that we are."

"We've used all our force, and they have hardly used their own force, yet we suffered more deaths than them," Chiri said, looking at Nehanda. "They have more guns and grenades, and we only have spear axes. You told the people that their enemy's bullets will turn to water, but you know that it won't happen, that they will die."

"Do you not think that I'm also scared?" Nehanda asked him. "I'm scared, but I understand that I'm their leader, their courage. If the two of us don't, who else can stand for them? Stand up as you stood for Kemu, as you did for me when I was weaker."

When Nehanda spoke Kemu's name, Chiri closed his eyes, and took a deep breath. "He was still young, and he never got the chance to see his children and grandchildren. He never got the chance to see the world around him, and he was just a sweet young fellow who only wanted nothing more but to smile."

"Don't let your thoughts eat your heart away," Nehanda told him. "Now he is in the land of the ancestors, and he is still that Kemu who wants nothing else but to smile. He has found peace and happiness and waits for us to join him one day."

"Why do we have to wait for death to finally find the perfect world? Whenever I close my eyes, I dream about what the world could be," Chiri said. "I see rainbows and beautiful mountains and hear laughter and an endless happiness. I wonder if we can ever create that world for our people."

Charwe looked up at the beautiful stars twinkling in the sky and wondered. There were hundreds and thousands of stars, and they all had been hanging in the sky, and not falling. The world was indeed mysterious. "We might not be able to create such a world, but we can at least try. Our hope must give us strength."

"Well, we can have hope, but how can that help when one is drowning and can't swim?" Chiri said, looking up at the stars. "But you might be right, it's good to have hope. Perhaps one day we will all laugh, and think back to these times," Chiri said, then laughed a bit. "Imagine a whole new world with dazzling beauty and magic. A world without darkness and tears, only light and laughter."

"Do you know of a pool named Peace?" Charwe asked. "Perhaps when this is all over, I will take you to the pool."

21

The Falling Bones

Nehanda looked up at the sky and noticed the dark clouds that were gathering overhead as the sun had been setting. She had just received the news of the pursuing European army. It had been shortly after she had received the news of the death of Chief Mashayamombe, and the capture of his spiritualist, Kaguvi Gumboreshumba.

"You are the witch," a thin voice took Nehanda from her thoughts. She turned and saw a young boy behind her, barely six years old.

"No, I'm not a witch. Those who take things that do not belong to them are the witches," Nehanda told him. "They do all the bad things, and then feast you with lies so that you turn your backs on your own guardians."

The mother of the boy then hurried to him, and held him under her arm, as if she was afraid Nehanda would harm him.

"Do not talk to my son, you'll corrupt him with your talk of rebellion and witchery," the woman said.

"I am your Mhondoro," Nehanda reminded the woman with a stern expression. "Why do you speak to me with such disrespect?"

"Because it is a choice that I've made in my life, to follow no one but Christ our saviour," the woman said. "I do not follow the old ways anymore. I've been baptised into a new life."

"I'm not forbidding you from doing whatever you want or to follow whomever you want. A heart is a tree, it grows where it wants to grow," Nehanda said. "This Jesus, he is the same as the creator and all…"

"He is different from you," the woman said. "He loves us and wants us to be happy. He wants the war to end, and for peace to conquer. You don't, you want us to keep on forcing our boys to go to war."

"Do you think I don't want the war to end," Nehanda asked her. "The forest only gives to those who tire. Peace will never come with us sitting on our hands. It can only come once the white man knows his place."

"You are preaching the wrong message," The woman said. "Preach repentance, not war. People should have peace, and they must learn to pray."

"I cannot stop, I have to defend this land they want to steal from us," Nehanda told her. "Tell me, what do you do when someone cuts your ear with a bakatwa?"

"I'll turn so that the man can cut the other one," the woman said. "Vengeance can never solve anything, but it will only make things worse. Cut his ear and he will cut your hand, and then you'll cut his hand, and it will go on until you kill each other."

"I am a Mhondoro, and I speak with the voice of the creator, Mwari himself. He sent me to protect the people, to lead them in this war and to end this carnage and stop all the suffering."

"How do you know, Charwe," the woman asked. "How do you know if it's indeed the creator who is speaking through you? What if it's a bad spirit, hungry for blood, hungry for war? Have you ever really thought about it?"

"I don't have to think about it, because I know what I am," Nehanda told her. "You clearly do not know what you are. Your new saviour might be good, but I want you to always remember that he is theirs, and not yours. You don't share your culture or blood with this man, but they do. They tell you to be as good as he is, but they do not do it themselves. They've come up with a strategy to weaken us. When war comes, who do you think this new saviour will favour, you or his own people?"

"Unlike you, he doesn't take sides. He is for us all, we are all equal in his eyes," the woman said, then turned to Nehanda. "Save yourself Charwe, before it's too late." The woman then made a sign of the cross, grabbed her child, and walked away from Nehanda.

Nehanda took deep breaths, trying to calm herself. A storm was now brewing within her. She feared that she was now losing the people, slowly becoming their enemy.

"You look grim today," Meda's voice took her from her thoughts.

She turned to him and saw the grin on his face.

"Have you not heard?" she asked him. "Wilson's last stand. The king of Mthwakazi is dead. An infantry of five hundred armed Europeans are on the march towards our territory. They want justice for their Native Commissioner, Pollard."

"Is that what you fear, Nyaka?" he said. "Is your faith so little? Our ancestors are with us, as they have always been. We have nothing to fear."

"Some of the villagers do not want the protection of the ancestors anymore," she told him. "They speak of the greatness of the God of the Europeans. He is a God who saves souls from condemnation, a God who lifts the poor from the dust."

"Why do you falter?" he said, as he held her cheeks. "Don't worry about anything else. Chiri is gathering up an army to repel these invaders. Have you forgotten what I told you? I believe you are sacred. I believe in you."

"They blame me, Meda," she told him. "They say I ordered the death of Pollard. They whisper that I'm the one who brought the war to them. They blame me for the drought and the rinderpest."

"I've heard songs about you from distant villages," Meda told her. "They say that you ride to battle with lions at your back. That you are invisible to the bullets of the white man. These songs might not be entirely true, but at least, it is giving them strength to resist. There will be those that will remember, those that will keep on singing the songs. You are the mother of liberation."

Meda lifted Charwe's chin with his hand, so that she would look directly into his eyes, so that through them she could see that he truly believed in her.

"I've gathered up the men," they heard Chiri's voice, as he walked up to where they had been standing. "We've to go and address them before we send them to war."

Nehanda turned to Chiri and nodded, then walked with him to where the fighters were gathered. She was surprised to see that they came in their hundreds. They all had their weapons, their spear axes and bows. Masvi also stood with his group of fighters, holding their rifles in hands.

All of them turned to Nehanda and Chiri and went quiet to hear what their leaders had to tell them.

Chiri was the first to deliver his speech. "Brothers, now we stand for one last fight to defend our territory. I'm sure you've heard of the tales of Wilson's last doom on the shores of Shangani. The amaNdebele King, Lobengula died, but on his own accord, not of his enemies. After his capital was captured, he fled north, and still the Europeans hunted him down. They wanted to kill him, but his warriors never allowed that to happen. They attacked and killed them all to the last man, Allan Wilson. Many of them died, but those brave men fought, even if they knew of their impending doom. We can defend our territory just as much as they defended their own king. Brave warriors! Right now as I speak, the Europeans are on the march, coming to take what is ours and to kill us all. We should not allow them. That is why we are standing here, now, to prepare to repel them. We may be outgunned, but we have something they don't—courage, unity, and knowledge of our terrains!" Chiri's voice was heard echoing throughout the village. "We will use that to our advantage. We will strike from the shadows, unleash our strength, and show them that we are a powerful dynasty, never to be tempered with."

His words ignited a new fire within his warriors' hearts, strength to fight for their homes and their people.

Nehanda stepped forward and gave her speech to the warriors. "Do not fear, for the greatest spirits of this land are with us. Mwari, the creator himself, is with us. Murenga Pfumojena Sororenzou, the lord of war, will lead us in spirit. This is his war, therefore it shall be known by those that will come after us as the Chimurenga war! Lift up your spear axe and prepare, for we are about to depart for war. Bees sting and they sting for sure."

"Murenga has awakened!" Meda gave out a war cry, as he raised his spear axe before the fighters.

"Murenga has awakened!" The other warriors raised their own spear axes after him, and indeed, the great spirit of war had awaked. The people then rose up into a war song.

Tora huta hwako toda kuenda dzinoruma, nyuchi dzinoruma, dzinoruma!

22

The war of Murenga

Under the cover of darkness, Chiri and his warriors stealthily moved through the forest, barely making a sound.

With a swift hand gesture, Chiri signalled his warriors to take their positions. They crouched low, blending seamlessly with the shadows, awaiting their enemies to draw close.

Chiri crouched low in the dense undergrowth, his heart pounding in his chest. The air was thick with tension as he peered through the leaves, waiting for the approaching troops, the men that wanted to take his home.

Masvi was also with them, alongside his fifty men armed with rifles.

Meda was right by Chiri's side. They exchanged glances, wordlessly acknowledging the dire situation they faced. But their resolve remained unshaken.

As the enemy soldiers drew closer, Chiri's heart pounded in his chest. He could hear them as they approached, and the air was thick with tension. This was their moment. He was waiting for them to come into view, so he would catch them unaware and unleash his barrage of arrows.

Catching Chiri with surprise, the first shots rang out, tearing through the air like thunder.

Bullets whizzed past, and one narrowly missed Chiri himself. It seemed the pursuing army knew that Chiri had been hiding with an army in the thicket. They had made the first move.

The sound of gunfire echoed through the forest, mingling with the cries of pain and defiance. Chiri turned and saw that some of his men had already fallen, before they had been aware that the fighting had commenced.

"Start the fire!" Chiri then gave out a command to his men, as he notched an arrow onto his bowstring and let it fly. Before it had reached its target, he had already notched another arrow and another. Arrows were now flying like a swarm of locusts, cutting through the forest. Most of the arrows found their targets with deadly precision, but it was also the same for the bullets from the enemies.

The Europeans had maxim guns with them, which they turned on. They unleashed a torrent of bullets, cutting through the foliage and tearing into many of the warriors.

Chiri turned for the cover of a tree, and he could feel the sound of the bullets sinking deep into the trunk. The deafening roar of the guns drowned out the sounds of battle, and Chiri's heart sank as he saw his comrades fall one by one, their bodies limp and lifeless.

For a moment, the maxim guns silenced, and at that instant, Chiri himself shouted for his warriors to stand from their cover and fight with spear axes.

All stood their ground and charged after the enemy, even as bullets whizzed past them.

The forest became a chaotic battleground, with arrows, bullets flying, swords and spear axes clashing.

The forest echoed with the sounds of clashing steel and the cries of the wounded. Chiri screamed as he spun his spear axe through the air, cutting a hand, and then a head, anything that was close to him. Each movement was calculated, each strike aimed to disarm or incapacitate.

Even others who had been fighting turned to glance at their chief as he moved swiftly with his spear axe, seamlessly transitioning from defence to offence, striking with great speed.

Chiri's skill became evident to all who witnessed it, and it would surely be sung for years to come. It was as if his spear axe was part of his arm, something he had been born holding.

He gave more courage to his warriors, and they fought valiantly, their determination unwavering. They pushed forward, driving the enemy back, and it seemed victory was within their grasp.

But as the battle raged on, Chiri's heart pounded when an arrow nearly took his life after passing right by his ear. Another arrow flew, and it struck through the throat of one of his warriors. He couldn't understand?

Meda ran to him and lowered him down for cover.

"Where are the arrows coming from?" Meda asked, seemingly confused. The Europeans never fought with arrows.

"From that cliff," Chiri pointed out to it. Meda looked and saw many men who were not part of their own army. Chief Matope stood amidst them garbed in his golden robe and mounting his horse. Mutimumwe was also next to him on his own horse, his eyes gleaming with contempt.

The realisation hit Chiri and Meda like a thunderbolt. Chief Matope's men had joined the European army, and had surrounded them all with their spear axes, arrows and guns. Now, their combined forces outnumbered Chiri's warriors, and the tide of the battle began to turn against them.

Meda never lost sight of Mutimumwe. Chief Matope and his men had left, and he was on the cliff alone, overlooking the battle on his horse. Meda swore to himself right then that he was going to kill that betrayer. Clutching his bow and arrow, he started running towards that hill.

Chiri was still trying to figure out a plan to free his men from the trap they were now in. With each passing moment, his people fell, pierced by arrows that seemed to rain down from the heavens. The forest echoed with the cries of pain and anguish. They were all falling down quickly, as the arrows seemed to come from all directions. Chiri knew he had to decide swiftly if he wanted to save his remaining men.

As he tried thinking of what to do, an arrow then stabbed him right on the shoulder, and it sank deep into his bone. Gritting his teeth against the searing pain in his shoulder, Chiri rallied his men, urging them to retreat, to cut their way out of the trap.

Their once fierce charge turned into a desperate retreat, as they fought their way through the chaos of the battlefield. Arrows whistled past them, finding their mark in the unfortunate few who couldn't evade the deadly rain.

Chiri's mind raced, searching for a path to safety. He knew that if he didn't act swiftly, he was going to die with his remaining warriors. With a heavy heart, he made the agonising choice to leave behind his other comrades.

After running through many raining arrows, Meda finally got close to Mutimumwe. That coward was not even fighting. He was just standing on his horse, overlooking the battle. Even if he wanted to, he never was really any good at fighting.

Meda stretched his arrow, then released it. The arrow went through Mutimumwe's chest, and he dropped from his horse and rolled down the cliff. Meda ran down to where Mutimumwe had rolled. He saw the man, screaming and bleeding from where the arrow had pierced him.

Mutimumwe was filled with dread when he saw Meda walking towards him, with an arrow in his hand.

"Mercy," he begged. "Please, mercy. I'm bleeding, I will die. Please help me."

"You always acted like you were clever at court," Meda said. "Always quarrelling like a woman."

"Please, mercy," he begged.

"You are a disgrace, Muti," Meda said. "I saw you that day, and I marked you. You pushed Kemu so that he would confront the commissioner, and now you are here, fighting against your own people. What was the price, huh? A horse? A robe of gold? You were always the betrayer from the very beginning. When we went to the station to capture the commissioner, it was already deserted. Someone had forewarned them to escape. All this time I had been wondering who it had been."

"I...I didn't want to! I swear!" Muti cried, his voice trembling. "It was... it was Masvi! It was Masvi. He put me to it. He's the one who warned the officers."

Meda tightened his stretch on his arrow and pointed it right at Mutimumwe. "You lie."

"No, it's the truth," Mutimumwe swore, his whole body shaking. "He works with them, employed as an officer. He promised the Europeans that he would deliver the Hwata chief to them, alive. I swear on my very life."

Meda never wanted to believe that any of what this bastard was saying was true. Masvi was one of the people that strongly wanted the commissioner to die. He couldn't possibly betray them. He couldn't.

As he had been battling with his thoughts, Meda remembered that he last saw Masvi as soon as the war had started. He was supposed to be close to him and Chiri. He had disappeared, probably gone to signal Matope to close in with his army.

Meda's breath came in shallow as the realisation came to him. Chiri, his chief, he thought, as he lowered his bow. He was probably in danger.

Without thinking twice about it, he left Muti languishing in his own pain and ran off to look for his chief before it was any too late.

Chiri himself was paces away, trying to hide from the arrows and bullets, his own wound killing him with pain.

He managed to slide through a dense undergrowth, the pain in his shoulder throbbing. Blood was gushing out, and for a moment, he felt like going back to the fighting and let someone kill him to end his pain.

The forest seemed to close in around him, as if nature itself conspired to impede his escape. Was it the ancestors? He wondered. No, it could not be them, they would have helped his men in the battlefield. Perhaps the ancestors themselves had been confused on which side to take. They were fighting against each other.

When he thought he had escaped the fighting, he found himself once again surrounded by screams and flying bullets and arrows. Chiri's heart pounded in his chest as he tried to make sense of the chaos unravelling before him. The sounds of screams and clashing steel echoed through the air, mingling with the heavy thuds of his own footsteps. His torn cloth scraped against his injured shoulder, causing searing pain, but his focus remained fixed on survival.

"Come, my Chief," the voice beckoned urgently, tugging at Chiri's senses. He turned swiftly, his heart pounding within his chest, only to find one of his trusted warriors standing before him. The soldier's face was etched with determination, lines of dirt and sweat marking his features.

"There's a place for you to hide," the soldier declared, his voice urgent yet filled with a deep sense of loyalty. "Be quick, you won't survive out here."

Relief washed over Chiri like a cool stream, momentarily numbing the ache in his weary limbs. He allowed the soldier to take hold of his arm, supporting him as they moved through the treacherous terrain. The soldier's grip tightened around Chiri's spear axe, a silent promise to protect his chief at all costs.

Together, they managed to escape the battlefield, the carnage and chaos growing more distant with each step.

Chiri felt a surge of relief when he saw that the soldier was leading him into a cave, a refuge from the madness.

As they entered the cave, Chiri felt a sudden pain in his side, where a bullet had grazed him. He stumbled and fell to the ground, clutching his wound.

He then looked up and saw a familiar face standing over him, holding a gun, pointing it right at him. It was Masvi, his very own army commander. But his expression was cold and cruel, and his eyes burned with malice, one Chiri had never seen before.

"Masvi, what is this? What are you doing?" Chiri gasped, disbelief and fear filling his voice. He raised his hands in a futile gesture of surrender, his mind reeling from the shock of the betrayal.

"You should have listened to me, Chiri," Masvi sneered, his voice dripping with scorn. "You should have never challenged the settlers, never started this rebellion. Now your men are being slaughtered like animals, and you've run away like a coward."

"I'm your chief, Masvi. I made you my army commander," Chiri said, trying to reason with him. "You wouldn't dare kill me."

Masvi smiled wickedly, his finger tightening on the trigger. "I'm not stupid, I won't kill you. They want you alive, not dead. I'm sorry, my chief, but the instinct of a hyena in the savanna is to survive. That's what I'm simply doing, just trying to survive."

Masvi pointed his gun at Chiri's chest, forcing him to drop to his knees. One of Masvi's men tied his hands behind him with a very thick rope. Masvi then lowered his gun, and commanded his men to take Chiri up, and walked with him outside. "The war will end when I hand you over to one of the generals. That is where I'm taking you now."

The war was still raging on, and Chiri could hear screams and gunfire in the night. The air itself was thick with smoke.

"What will your descendants make out of your betrayal to your own people, what songs will they sing about you?" Chiri asked, looking up at Masvi who had now been on top of his own horse.

"Only those who survive sing the songs, and only the cunning and the devious are the ones who survive," Masvi told Chiri, as his horse started walking. "And also, do not worry, songs don't matter. You always sing about Shayachimwe the conqueror, but does that make his bones roar in the grave?"

"And his legacy? The dynasty that Shayachimwe fought to build?" Chiri said, as he stumbled, Masvi's men shoving him forward. "What you are doing is wrong, it will anger the ancestors!"

"The ancestors are angry all the time, and besides, they are dead. Tell me, by what right do the dead judge the living? We live in completely separate worlds, and their opinions are not a concern to us."

"They walked on this soil before us, Masvi," Chiri said. "They are our guardians, our very protectors."

"Protectors? Come on Chiri, you are a clever man, you can't possibly believe that," Masvi said. "Do you honestly think that they will come to your rescue? No one can save you, dear Chiri. Not the ancestors, not God. None of them are here, only you. You can save yourself, but how do you do that when you are chained?"

"You think you are clever don't you!" Chiri spat. "You think that your wise sayings will justify your treachery. We all might do wrong but there is only one rule above all else, one rule every man should follow, to protect our own kind. Our kind must be our pride."

"Protect our kind, you say. I've done less harm than what you've done," Masvi lectured Chiri. "You started a war that you knew you wouldn't win. You've only made things worse for the people, along with your Nehanda. The villages have been destroyed, along with the fields, people are losing their lives as we speak. The people are now hungrier than they were before, and all this because of what, your pride?"

"I hate you, Masvi," Chiri told him. As he was being dragged, he stepped his right leg into a pile of fresh dung, and he cursed.

"Do you hate me, or my piercing words, which are nothing but the honest truth?" Masvi asked him. "It was stupid of you to fight against the white man. You knew that he was more powerful, yet you insisted on fighting anyway."

"I was made a chief, and unlike you, I understand my duties. I understand that I have to defend my people from the enemy, even when I know I won't win. A good leader fights to his grave."

"And also you must remember, a good leader fights with wisdom, which you certainly failed to use. Imagine an eland grazing in a field, alongside her children. She then realises that a pride of lions is approaching them. The eland then runs after the lions to chase them away from the children, even though it knows that the lions have more canine teeth, claws and strength. Tell me, what do you think will happen to the eland?"

Chiri remained quiet, even though he knew the answer.

Masvi spat out the answer. "The lions will devour her and eat her to the last bone. And when the eland is gone, who will be left to protect her children from the pride? A wise leader knows when to fight and when to flee. He doesn't just choose to fight to the grave."

Chiri felt a cold dread in his chest, and tears stung his eyes. He turned to look away, his breaths now shallow. "I was fighting a war on the right side, defending my people. I followed my duties, along with my rules. I don't care if I die, Masvi, as long as I know that I tried."

"I'm sorry to tell you this now, but a war is a game, a gamble," Masvi whispered. "You don't have to always play a fair game, you know, following the rules, and doing what is expected of you. You don't win that way. The Europeans are winning because they wield the mind like a sword, while your pathetic self clings to your spear axe like a stick."

"It will only be for a little while, but a time will come when the people shall rise and fight again, and eventually win," Chiri said. "It might be in a month or in ten years, but there shall come a day when we shall be the winning side."

"Even when the black man fights and retakes power from the whites, it will never be the righteous or decent one that shall rule thereafter," Masvi said. "It's the cunning, the devious and the plotter; it is the man who won't follow the rules, the one that doesn't care about the consequences of his actions. To rule, you must know the true meaning of power, dear Chiri."

"There shall come a day when the bird will break the trap, Masvi, when you'll realise that you are not as clever as you think."

"I didn't say I was clever, but maybe I am a bit more than you. You are the one in chains, not me. I know where to use and to save my strength," Masvi said. "But you are right, a day might come, but lucky enough, it's not today. For now, I will just try my best to survive, to save myself from death."

Masvi's horse halted when a rustling sound came from the bushes. Masvi narrowed his eyes to clearly see what it was. From the shadows, Meda emerged, his face twisted with anger. He moved swiftly, his bow drawn, and an arrow notched, ready to fly.

"What are you doing, Masvi?" Meda asked with fury. "That's your chief, you imbecile. Are you not ashamed?"

Masvi just sneered, his grip tightening on the reins. He just looked at Meda as if looking at someone pathetic, worthless.

"Let him go, Masvi," Meda spat out. "Let him go or I swear this arrow will stab through your skull."

Then, a sharp crack of a gunshot echoed through the forest. Meda gasped, his body jerking as the bullet tore through his leg. The pain was immediate and excruciating. His bow slipped from his grasp as he crumpled to the ground, screaming in agony.

"You should've just shot the arrow the moment you got the chance," Masvi laughed, then turned to his men. "Take him too. He is the one who took the command of the witch to kill Pollard."

23

The Union Jack

A piercing scream escaped Charwe's lips as the dreadful news reached her ears. They had lost the war and her brother, her dear Chiri, had been taken hostage by the enemy.

It was her own first-born son that had relayed this word to her, in the cave where she had been hiding.

"As we speak now, the warriors that survived are being lined up, interrogated and being executed afterwards," Hungwariri told her. "They say they won't stop until they find information about you. They say you murdered Henry Pollard, and they want you to answer to that." Those words hit her like an arrow on her heart. She then turned to look at the fire, tears streaming from her eyes. "Is there anything else to do?"

Hungwariri looked into her eyes, and he could see that there was no hope in them. He then realised what had been on her mind, what she intended to do.

"No, you shall not. There is still time, you can save yourself," the boy told her. "You can run away, far away from this place, where they will never find you, where no one will know your name."

"But that won't stop them from tormenting the villagers, will it? They won't stop until they find us," Charwe said. "I'm their guardian, I cannot flee the people. I am sworn to protect them. It's their lives that matter, not mine. I can only protect them by surrendering, by declaring defeat."

"This is our land, our gold, our people," Hungwariri protested. "Surrendering cannot be an option. We have to keep fighting. If it means we will all die, and then let's die, but you must live on, to continue the fight."

"What will we be fighting for, when the people themselves clearly don't know what they want?" Nehanda asked him. "The people already surrendered themselves. The people are slowly becoming what they are fighting. They are all changing, and some of them seem to enjoy it. The sad reality is that slaves forget who they once were. They easily bow down to their masters and learn to feel comfort in their oppression. The people think that the settlers are superior to them, and that they are nothing themselves. We've already been defeated, in our minds."

Nehanda then stood up and started walking out of the cave. "You must go now, to Tandi and Svotwa. They need you, Hungwa."

"I told you that day, mother," Hungwa said. "I will never leave you, never. They won't take you, while I'm here, while I'm still breathing."

"You'll be in danger as long as you are with me. They will kill you too, and I will curse the day that happens. Leave me, so I might put an end to the war I started. I know you are a stubborn little brat, but don't dare to follow me. Your siblings still need you, in this dark and unpredictable world. Hungwa, live up to your name, not in the wrong way. Never raise your hand to a woman, ever. Be kind, be gentle and always know that I love you, and I will never stop loving you."

"No, no, no, you can't go," the boy insisted, tears streaming down his cheeks, as his mother walked away. "You can't, they'll kill you."

She did not listen to him but continued walking towards the bush where the captured men were being interrogated.

She was leaving behind her son, and it pained her. Every step she took, she was walking further away from him, and perhaps would not see his smile ever again. She wanted to turn back to him, to look at his face for just one last time, but she kept her head stiff. She knew she would break the moment his eyes met hers.

Svotwa and Tandi were still waiting for her, so that she would take them back home. Would she ever take them back?

She was scared, but she knew that she had to give up the fight. The odds had not been on their side.

A gunshot echoed through the bush, along with some screams, but Nehanda was not moved. She kept walking to surrender to her enemy.

She then started walking amongst piles of dead bodies, and the smell of blood filled the air. She tried not to look at the dead people, but they were everywhere. There were just too many. Bodies of Europeans and natives on the ground.

The sad reality of war was that even when one side loses or wins, both sides suffer the same losses.

Most of the bodies had their eyes open. She could feel those eyes gazing at her as she walked, cursing her and blaming her for their deaths. Some of the bodies were moving, still alive.

"Nehanda, save me!" one of her men cried as he lay on the ground. Charwe turned to him. He had no leg and had two arrows sunk in his back. He was in great pain. "Just slit my throat open and save me from this pain."

Charwe could only look at him, then turned away, tears welling up in her eyes. She kept walking, never stopping.

Finally, from a distance, she could see the captured men lined up, surrounded by European soldiers with rifles and flashlights.

It seemed like they were being questioned, one by one. There were others who were lying on the ground, and they clearly had been shot. One boy was dragged to the front, where a stern officer interrogated him.

"Where is your master? Where is the witch Nyanda? Where is she hiding?" he shouted.

The boy stammered some vague words which Nehanda couldn't hear. He knew nothing, or maybe he was too loyal to betray their cause.

Either way, it didn't matter. The officer nodded to a soldier, who raised his gun.

"Stop!" Nehanda said, as she appeared from the shadows of the forest. "I am the witch that you hunt for."

The soldiers turned their guns and pointed out to her, and she dropped down to her knees.

"Stop killing the boys. I've come to surrender," Charwe said. "I wish for the war to end."

The officer, Selous, smiled wickedly. "Well, well, well. Look who decided to show up. The hero of the revolution and the champion of freedom."

He gestured to his men. "Arrest her! Take her away!"

The soldiers rushed to grab her, and she offered no resistance. She was handcuffed and pushed away. They dragged her all the way back to her village, so that she would announce to the people herself that the war had ended.

Nehanda had her hands raised and tied to the back of her head all the way to the main village, and she was now feeling a throbbing pain on her arms. When they got to the village, the streets were deserted. The only sound was the wind blowing through the trees.

The women and children had all been hiding behind walls and barrels. Their eyes followed the men holding Charwe as they walked into their villages, wondering what they were going to do. In the shadows, some of the villagers cried, some of them prayed, some of them cursed, as the footsteps of their enemies echoed off the walls.

Charwe herself could see them hiding in the shadows, their faces filled with fear. They then reached the centre of the village, where there were other men standing, and they had Chiri. He had also been in chains and seemed quite wounded. Chiri had a lot of blood on his chest.

Charwe wanted to run and hug her brother, but she couldn't.

The officer then walked to the centre of the village and looked around at the empty huts and the silent streets.

He knew that the people were hiding and were watching from the shadows.

The officer, Selous, raised his arms in a gesture of peace. "I've brought you your enemies," he said, in the native tongue that all could hear. "These evil men started a rebellion to kill young boys and men all for nothing. They are cold blood murderers, and they shall stand in the court of law and answer for all their crimes. We are taking them so that we can all live in peace and harmony."

"I am Chiripanyanga Hwata, your chief, and an evil man," Chiri confessed, his voice croaking. He was trying his very best to hold back his tears. It was very clear that he had been forced to say what he was saying. "I've come before you all to confess my transgressions. I swore to protect you all and lead you to prosperity, but instead, I've killed your children and your husbands, and I've caused plagues to fall upon your lands. I've allowed a witch to whisper in my ear and chased away good friends from this land. I hope you find a place in your hearts to forgive me."

"No," Nehanda shook her head as she cried. "No, that's a lie! Chiri did nothing wrong, he was just trying to protect his people, he was just—"

"Silence, witch!" the officer barked, "My men say you killed Pollard."

"No, no, she did not," Meda, trembling, pushed himself to his feet, despite the throbbing pain from his wounded leg. "She did not kill him. It was me. I held the blade. I'm the one who slit his throat."

Selous turned his gaze to Meda. "And who the hell gave you permission to speak?"

Meda then looked down and admitted in a low whisper. "No one." Those words seemed to have drained him of the little strength that remained to him. Despite his desperate struggle to remain on his feet, the pain overtook him. With a guttural cry, he collapsed to his hands and knees, his breaths coming in ragged gasps.

"You look like you are in a lot of pain," the officer said. "I'm generous enough to put you out of your misery. Remember my kindness in the afterlife."

Without a second's hesitation, he raised his rifle and took aim. The sound of the trigger pulling was almost drowned out by the sudden silence that filled the air. The bullet pierced through Meda's skull with a sickening crack, and then his body dropped to the ground with a thud.

Charwe's screams tore through the silence, as blood pooled beneath Meda, dark and thick, and mocking all the memory of the pool named peace.

The officer ignored the screams and raised his voice to address the people hiding in the shadows. "You heard your chief, you heard of his transgressions. Why keep fighting for the man who clearly hates you all. He has declared that you all must end this foolish resistance. I am offering you a truce. Lay down your arms and surrender and all this fighting will stop. Your village shall start anew under the arms of Chief Matope, and the administration of the Rhodesian government. We promise to help you through the drought and rinderpest. I am giving you a chance and this is your only chance."

The villagers looked at him, and at Meda's body on the ground. They knew they had no choice. They had to surrender.

One by one, the men stepped out of the shadows and laid down their weapons.

It was on this day that the Hwata territory was captured, and a Union Jack was tied onto a tree.

The tides of war were shifted, and eventually, the resistance quickly died out throughout the lands.

The blacks had been defeated across the whole land that stretched between Zambezi and Limpopo. The land was now called Rhodesia after Cecil John Rhodes, for it was now his. Everything belonged to him, from the gold to the very people.

He had crushed all those that had led the wars, both in Matabeleland and Mashonaland. The various chiefs and their 'wizards' and 'witches' had all been arrested and were awaiting fair trial for the massacre they caused in the war they started.

The great and feared Ndebele Kingdom had been crushed with the rest of them. Their king, Lobengula had died of a fever as he was trying to escape the pursuing European army. Their leader in war, Mlimo, had been killed, and most of their men and boys had perished in the war.

24

An Oath of Return

In their confinement, the rebel leaders were treated accordingly. They were starved and kept under harsh conditions as they awaited their trial. Others became so pale and thin that the lines of their rib cages could be seen.

Kaguvi Gumboreshumba was also imprisoned and charged with the murder of a police officer.

Charwe found herself wishing she had not been initiated. Maybe things would've been different for her.

She closed her eyes and imagined Meda swimming in the pool named Peace.

He is still there, she told herself. *He is still swimming in that pool along with all the spirits of those who were gone for so very long.*

The cell was dark and filled with the irritating singing of mosquitoes. She sat there as they feasted on her blood, making her life more miserable than it had been. The cold seeped into her bones, chilling her to the core. Charwe wrapped her arms around herself, seeking solace in her own embrace.

The darkness enveloped her like a shroud. She felt a sharp pain in her ribs, where one of the soldiers had kicked her during the arrest. She wondered if they had broken anything. She hoped not. She needed to be strong.

She found herself thinking of Chiri and his own wound. She wondered how he was feeling and felt sorry for him.

She felt abandoned and she needed comfort. She wanted to be at the pool named Peace.

Charwe found herself also thinking of Svotwa, and her cheerful smile. She thought of Tandi, and his unbearable snores. She missed her children.

She knew that she needed nothing to worry about for they were safe, as long as Hungwa was with them. She smiled when she thought about her strong firstborn son, her brave boy. Charwe started singing a song she remembered only in her ancient memories. *Tovera mudzimu dzoka!* She sang, as she sat all alone, shivering in the cold. *Mudzimu dzoka!*

Her memories took her back in the past to when she had been sitting with her father, Murenga. This had been about a millennium ago.

They had been atop a hill, singing the song.

Tovera mudzimu dzoka! She sang with her father. The sun was setting over the hills, casting a golden glow over the land. Everything in that moment was beautiful, sweet and peaceful.

She was with her father, overlooking the men that were working beneath the hill, cutting rocks into blocks and piling them up, one on top of the other.

Her brothers, Chaminuka and Chishawatu were overlooking the work, and directing the workers with gestures and whistles. They were building the mighty kingdom of Dzimbabwe, the great house of stone.

"Will this kingdom be as great and prosperous as Mapungubwe?" Nehanda asked her father.

The soft plucks of the mbira, and sound of shaking seed gourds danced within her mind, as her father wrapped his arm around her shoulders.

"Yes, it will go on to survive for centuries, I'm sure of it. I'm also sure of the fact that it won't last," Murenga said, as a bateleur eagle landed on a branch of a tree that was near them. "A bird can fly up as high as the clouds in the sky, but it will always land on the ground or a branch. Nehanda, you must know that everything that begins always has its end, as the sun rises and falls, a man is born and dies. As Mapungubwe fell, this kingdom we are starting will also fall and see its end."

"I will never let that happen," Nehanda replied boldly to her father. "I will always fight for my people, even when I'm long dead. We can do that, right? We can live on as spirits to fight for the people. We can live a thousand lives, in a thousand generations, guiding our generations till the end of time itself."

"Yes, we can. We are the Mhondoro, the true seeds of Tanganyika, the land of creation. We are the great lion spirits of Guruuswa, and the magic of that land flows in our veins. We can be born into this world again," Murenga told her. "But you must certainly know that if you want to fight with the people in the last days of the kingdom, it will be your burden to watch the fall of everything that I'm building now, and I won't lie, the burden will be heavy."

I'm here, Baba, Nehanda Charwe Nyakasikana thought in her mind, as she trembled in the cold of her cell. *I'm here as I promised, and what you said is true, the burden is indeed heavy.* Nehanda found herself wailing, crying loudly in her anguish.

"You shall watch the kingdom falling," Murenga's words danced within her. "You shall watch the bones crumble to the ground."

"If the bones fall, will they ever rise again?" she asked him.

"Perhaps they will, perhaps they won't," he told her. "Perhaps the people will despise us; perhaps they shall cut their ties with us, with the power of Guruuswa, the power that flows in their veins. Perhaps they will find a new life, perhaps they will denounce their totems, forget us in their memories, and we will only be strangers to them."

Charwe's tears trickled down her cheeks, and they seemed a bit warmer than the breeze tormenting her.

She sat on the cold, hard floor of the cell, her back against the damp wall. The only light came from a small window high above, barely enough to see the outlines of the bars and the door. She could hear the faint sounds of other prisoners, but no one spoke to her. She was alone.

25

The Trial

Nehanda walked into the courtroom, hands bound in chains. There were many people in the room, all waiting to hear the court proceedings. Some of the people were her fellow natives, but they all had been dressed in the clothes of the settlers.

In front of everyone else, there was an old man with a stern look and strange white hair, sitting on a high bench. He was Judge Watermayor of the High Court of Salisbury, the new established capital of the settlers.

Nehanda was escorted by two guards to her dock. The prosecutor, a young and eager lawyer, stood at a podium with his stack of papers. Herbert Hayton Castens Esquire was the public prosecutor acting on behalf of her majesty, the Queen of England.

Judge Watermayor banged his gavel and called for order.

"Silence in the court!" he shouted. "This is the case of the Crown versus Nyanda, a self-proclaimed spiritualist and also a rebel leader. She is charged with the murder of Henry Hawkins Pollard, a Native Commissioner of Mazoe, on the 19th of June 1896. How do you plead, Nyanda?"

Nehanda had not understood anything that the judge had said, until a translator interpreted it to her. Nehanda looked at the judge with a steady gaze. She then replied in her own native language.

"I do not recognise your authority over me or my people. You are invaders and oppressors who have stolen our land and cattle, who have killed our men and raped our women, who have forced us to work for you and pay taxes to you. You have no right to judge me or accuse me of anything. I am innocent of your charges." The translator repeated Nehanda's words in English.

The judge shook his head. "You are not here to make political statements or to deny the facts. You are here to answer for your crimes. You have been identified by several witnesses as the leader that commanded the execution of Mr. Pollard. Do you deny this?" Nehanda remained quiet, even after the translator told her the words in the language she understood. The judge sighed, then he signalled the prosecutor to bring up one of the witnesses.

Nehanda's eyes followed the witness slowly, as he walked to stand at the front of the courtroom. The man was no other than Masvi, their very own army commander, the one who had fought next to Chiri.

He was very different from the man she knew. He was wearing a black suit and a black tie with stripes. He was one of them now, she realised. He had always been one of them.

The judge asked him to raise his right hand and hold a big book in his left hand.

"I swear to tell the truth, the whole truth and nothing but the truth, So help me God," Masvi repeated after the translator. Everyone was quiet to listen to this witness, Masvi, son of Gotora.

"State your name and occupation for the record, please," the prosecutor, H.H Castens said.

"My name is Masvi Nyandoro, a black watcher," the witness said.

"And how do you know the prisoner, Witch Nyanda?" the prosecutor asked.

"I worked as a spy under her army which she formed to start the war alongside her chief," Masvi said. "As far as I know, she was cruel and violent, even when it came to how she delivered her justice."

"What do you mean when you say she was cruel and violent? Can you give us an example of how she delivered her justice with her cruelty?" H.H Castens asked.

"Yes, I can. I can clearly recall the day. I was there when she killed Mr. Pollard. I saw it with my own eyes," Masvi said.

"Tell us exactly what it is you saw," the prosecutor, H.H Castens inquired.

"They dragged Pollard and threw him on the ground. He was bleeding as they had thrashed him, but he was still alive. He begged for mercy, but they showed him none. She gave the order, and his head was chopped off. Nehanda watched, and she never flinched. She later commanded them to throw the body down a stream, to hide it." Masvi paused and looked straight at Nehanda.

"Your ancestors must be ashamed to hear you saying these things," Nehanda told him.

"Can you please be silent and let my witness finish what he has to say," the prosecutor instructed her at once. "Your turn will come, witch Nyanda."

"Why should they be ashamed, dear Charwe," Masvi stared at her. "I'm not the one that forced little boys to war, and I'm also not the one in chains, defeated."

Masvi then turned to the judge to finish off his narration. "As I was saying, Nehanda led little boys to war, and she led to the rift between the blacks and the whites. She has no understanding of both unity and equality. She wants to throw the people back a thousand years, to the world where she truly belonged, that's if her claims are to be believed at all."

"And which claims are these?" the prosecutor asked.

"She believes that she possesses magical abilities, that she can speak with God, and that she once lived thousands of years ago, perhaps a thousand lives," he explained. "She claims that she can make rain, though we are currently in the midst of the worst drought ever. She says it is you who came with the rinderpest and the drought and the locusts, building hatred towards you. She is a disruption to change. It seems she wants to throw the people back to a time where they were miserable and poor, when they used to live in trees and were not different from the monkeys."

"That would be all, Masvi. Thank you for your testimony, you have been very brave and honest," the prosecutor said, then turned to the judge. "No further questions, your honour."

"You sellout," Nehanda said, her gaze unwaveringly fixed on Masvi. "Everything I did was for the betterment of my people, for you and your family, and all your loved ones. Yet here you are, dining with strangers, forgetting that they won't be there by your side when you face your ancestors in the afterlife."

Masvi paused, his eyes meeting Nehanda's, and a flicker of pity crossed his face.

"Save yourself, Nehanda," Masvi challenged her. "Aren't you the hero of this story? The legendary Mhondoro we've all heard about in tales? Prove to us that your existence is more than just a mere myth." Nehanda swallowed hard, struggling to find the right words in response to Masvi's taunt.

"You can't save yourself, can you?" he continued, speaking in the native tongue, only for her to hear. "You were deceived, just as much as you deceived yourself, into believing that you are the incarnation of the Nehanda spirit. It's a figment of your imagination, a fabrication you clung to because you desperately wanted it to be true. But when your mental power fails to manifest in the real world, you realise it was all a lie—a deception that provided false hope."

"It's not a deception," Nehanda spoke with unwavering conviction. "I am Nehanda, the maneless white, daughter of Murenga Pfumojena—"

"Then prove it," Masvi interrupted. "Surely there must be something more than mere words. A crow may convince itself that it's a dove, but that can never change the colour of its feathers. It's simply a falsehood." Masvi then turned and walked out of the courtroom, blurring Nehanda's mind with his words.

"Order," the judge said as he banged his gavel to get Nehanda's attention, although half her mind was lost to what Masvi had just told her. "You are accused of the murder, Nyanda. Do you plead guilty?" the judge asked.

"I will not plead guilty, if you do not plead guilty," Nehanda said, now tears flowing down her cheeks. "I won't just stand here as you all try to prove to me that I'm the one who's wrong and lost, when I know for sure that I'm right. No one is accusing you of stealing our land, of raping the women. You traitors, you came as beggars disguised as traders, and now you want to bend us. You came as savage hyenas dressed in masks of innocent bushbucks. You are now placing me on trial for trying to defend my own land. If Pollard died, then he met fair judgement for trying to control the land that never belonged to him or his ancestors."

"There's nothing more to discuss here," Judge Watermayor said. "You killed Pollard, and you are willing to kill more of us. Witch Nyanda, you've been found guilty of the murder of Henry Hawkins Pollard. You will be sentenced to death by hanging."

Judge Watermayor then hit his gavel to pass his judgement.

26

The last supper

Nehanda sat down on the cold floor and looked around her familiar small cell, filled with filth and stink.

She was not going to stay in that prison for too long. Soon enough she would be reunited with her ancestors.

"I'm sorry to hear that you've been sentenced to death," she heard the voice of Father Richertz, as he walked to her cell. This had not been his first visit. "Even though the law finds you guilty, Nehanda, I assure you that the creator has already forgiven all your wrongdoings, and the only thing you have to do is to have faith in him."

"Is that what you tell yourselves?" Nehanda looked up at him. "Perhaps that's why you are so bold to steal things that do not belong to you; because you tell yourselves that you are already forgiven."

"I do not steal things that do not belong to me, I'm just a priest," Father Richertz said and crouched down to her. A crucifix hung down his neck. "I would lie if I said that my people are doing right by taking your land. I do not like what they are doing, because it is wrong. There are many evil people out there, but you must not be like them. You have a chance to be different and take a new path to walk through."

"If that's what you truly believe, then I think you are speaking with the wrong person," Nehanda told him. "You must be speaking with them, the evil men, and not me. I don't have a need to be different, because I'm already different from them, and mind you, I'm quite comfortable in my own path."

"I don't think you are. I'm here, speaking with you now, because I understand you need hope and courage," the priest told her. "The evil men out there don't want it; they don't believe in it. All they care about is their earthly wealth. They forget that we are just souls in a body, and that one day, they will leave the body."

"I'm dying tomorrow, what hope would I ever want?" Nehanda asked him. "My people have been defeated, and now the war has ended."

"Do you not think that it is good for the war to end?" the priest asked her. "There wouldn't be bloodshed and wailing, and the people would be at peace. The blacks and whites can actually live together; we all just need to understand that we are equal, and the main purpose of life is to love one another."

Nehanda smiled slightly. "If only it was that easy for men to live and love one another, things would've been different from the very beginning. Men have a desire for conflict, and it can never seem to end."

"Unfortunately, men are inseparable from sin. It is an infection, too hard to cure," the priest agreed with her. "It's only in the afterlife where we shall live in eternal peace, without the burden of sin. We would be in heavenly grace, in the comfort of our Lord and saviour."

"Have you ever seen him?" Nehanda asked the priest. "The saviour that you always tell me about?"

"No I haven't," father Richertz admitted. "I've read about him from a big special book called the bible. I made a choice to believe him because I know he is good. He walked on this earth about two thousand years ago, preaching the good news to the people of the world, giving them new courage and hope."

"I've heard stories about him too," Nehanda smiled at Father Richertz. "He is indeed a good man. He has given me the courage I need, the courage to face death without fear."

The priest was quite amazed and drew closer to Charwe with excitement, "Really?"

"When I thought about his story, I saw it to be more similar to mine. He died under the hands of his enemies, placing false accusations against him, and he died for the liberation of his people. His own people denounced him, saying he was not the messiah they needed. They turned their backs on him, just like some of my people turned their own backs on me. He died for his own people, and I will die for my own."

"I'm glad you've understood. Are you willing to take this journey, Nehanda?" the priest asked. "To accept him as your saviour and be baptised in his name, so that you can live in eternal peace, in heaven with him?"

"I can't," Nehanda said. "He is a foreigner to me. I know nothing about him except for the stories you tell me. You made your own choice to believe in him, and I believe I have the right to make my own. Perhaps he is real, but I think I prefer to live in eternal peace with my ancestors, the ones that I'm familiar with. I know for certain that they are real."

The priest was about to speak when she stopped him from speaking. "Save your energy, father. There was once a priest who tried to convert us, a long time ago, when I was Nyamhita. I recall his name quite well, Father Gonzalo da Silveria."

"What do you mean?" the priest couldn't understand. "Father Gonzalo was a missionary who died five centuries ago. How can you possibly know about him?"

"Because I'm me," Nehanda replied, then she closed her eyes, humming a song.

She had her final dream that night, which was very strange to her. She was standing near a small stream that ran into the Mukuvisi River. She was very thirsty, and wanted to drink from the river, but before she could, the ground moved and pushed her away from the stream. Disoriented, she spun around, witnessing in horror as the ground beneath her rose up and covered the stream. She realised that she now had been standing atop a small hill and the vast land around her was changing rapidly as the ground turned and ate up trees and rivers. Two bateleur eagles flew and landed on her shoulders.

The earth roared and trembled as massive and terrifying structures grew from the earth. Before her eyes, these structures grew taller than the small hill that she had been standing upon. They grew so tall that she thought they were going to touch the sky. They had destroyed everything that had once been standing there, and only a few trees remained in sight. In her life or in any of her past lives, she had never seen something like this.

Before she could comprehend what was unfolding before her eyes, she saw huge crowds looking up at her and waving their hands, cheering and calling out her name. Some were on their knees, praising her and speaking great of her name.

"The lady of freedom," they called her, "the liberator of the people."

She never understood what they were doing. She looked around and saw that this hill had been at a confluence of roads. The bateleur eagles had also been overlooking the scenery with their sharp gazes.

Underneath the shadow of these structures around her, and beyond the voices of the people praising her, she heard distant screams and gunfire. She looked in that distance, and saw mothers and children running and screaming, the air heavy with smoke. Some were on their knees, crying and choking.

The people praising her never seemed to notice everything that was going on behind them. They kept praising her and saying great things about her name and her legacy.

As she had been trying to understand everything, she realised that it was all happening on one side of the hill.

When she turned to look at the other side, a cooler breeze welcomed her. She realised that there were more trees on this side, and also less chaos. *This must be the afterlife*, she thought, for it was quite a beautiful scenery, with many trees of pink and purple flowers. Chirping birds filled the air in their hundreds, flapping their wings in the flowery scented gale. The people on this side were happier and less hungry and chaotic than those from the other side.

She herself would prefer to be on this side than the other.

She couldn't understand how they were the same people, divided by this hill that she was standing upon. She felt a bit of relief when she saw that there was a man standing a bit closer to her. Perhaps this person could explain all that was happening.

She wanted to walk to him, but then realised that she couldn't move, but only rotate at that point where she was standing, overlooking the whole landscape. She asked the people to help her, but they all didn't seem to hear her. She really couldn't understand anything and was only able to escape it all when she woke from her dream.

No dream had ever troubled her more than her last dream, her own last supper. Her cell was still dark, but the crowing of the cock reminded her that her last day had finally arrived.

27

The Execution

A war is coming!

Nehanda could still clearly hear the words of the madman in her mind, as she was being escorted by the guards out of her prison cell. She had been walking with Chiri that day, she remembered. It was well before she knew she was ever going to be a Nehanda.

She laughed to herself when she thought about it. They had all been warned before, by a ragged madman, and they all never thought much about it. They all said he was sick in the head, never knew what he was talking about.

If only they had known, if only.

Perhaps, it could have been different. But now, none of that mattered. Nothing could be undone. Charwe was now walking to her end.

Charwe blinked when the sunlight hit her eyes, making her squint and turn away, as she walked out into the prison yard.

She felt a surge of pain and relief, as if she was seeing the world for the first time. She had been in the darkness for a long time. She had forgotten what it was like to feel the warmth of the sun, the breeze on her skin and see the colours of the day.

A large crowd had already been gathered, waiting to witness her end.

She remembered the day of her initiation, when she walked out of her hut, with Meda by her side. She was just as scared as she had been now. Meda was with her then, and now she was standing alone. She had been walking to her rebirth then, and now she was walking to her death.

Nehanda turned her head to the people around her, and wondered how it had all gone wrong.

Nehanda looked from a white man to a black man and from black to a white man and from white man to black again; and she could hardly tell which was which.

They all looked the same. Her people had all removed their clothing, and they had new ones. They had thrown away their tongue and they now spoke in a new one. They had thrown away their culture and now they had found a new one. They all were kneeless men, and she now felt as if she was in a world where she never belonged.

She could only wonder what they had been thinking about. She knew that to most of them, she was a witch that had caused many people to die, a witch that deserved all that was happening to her.

She didn't care. She didn't care at all about what they thought about her, or about what names they gave her.

Their sharp gazes were never going to break her, for she was not a stranger to shame. She had failed her people, but she was not going to let shame bow her. She was not going to hide, for she was brave and unbowed. She was the great lion spirit of Nehanda.

In her mind, she told herself that she had no need to regret anything.

They were killing her, but she was also leaving a mark on the world. Many that were going to come after her would speak tales of her legacy. They would all know that she once lived, and she loved, and she fought, and had done all she was supposed to do. She did her best, so they would not forget her name.

Meda was waiting for her in the pool named Peace.

***

In that same hour, inside his dark and damp cell, Kaguvi Gumboreshumba leaned against a wall, feeling the cold stone against his skin. He had lost track of time and hope, waiting for his inevitable execution. Father Richertz was right next to him, telling him the good news of the gospel.

"Dismas was a criminal, just like you, Kaguvi," Father Richertz explained. "Dismas, the Good Thief, found salvation in his final moments. He recognised his own brokenness, repented from his sins. As he was promised, Jesus was with him in paradise the day he died. The question is, do you want to be in paradise after you die?"

Kaguvi looked into the priest's eyes, searching for a glimpse of truth and sincerity. He had heard many lies and promises before, and he wasn't sure if he still could take any more. He had failed his people, and now they were in the devil's spawn. He watched his own chief, Mashayamombe, die in his arms. He had watched his villages all destroyed by fire. He had tried fighting, but he failed miserably, and was captured, and taken away from his people. He had lost everything he cared about.

He didn't want any more assurances and broken promises, but there was something different about Father Richertz, something that made him want to believe him. Maybe it was the way he spoke with conviction and passion, or maybe he was the only one who showed him a little bit of care. He was the only one who visited, the only one who didn't give commands with anger. Maybe it was the way he offered him a chance to escape from his misery and despair, to find a new yet unexplored life beyond death.

"Is it good in paradise?" Kaguvi found himself asking. "Will I find happiness there?"

"That and many other things," the priest told him. "It's the most beautiful place ever, and there, you'll experience a profound sense of belonging and love. You'll see God face to face, and he'll wipe away every tear from your eyes. You'll have no more pain or sorrow or fear or guilt or shame. You'll be free from all the evil and injustice that have plagued this world. You'll be part of a new creation, where everything is good and perfect and glorious."

That was what Kaguvi had wanted to hear, about hope, about happiness, about peace and beauty. He felt a warm sensation in his chest, a spark of faith that ignited his soul. He wanted to believe that such a place existed, that he could go there too, that he could rest from all this suffering and uncertainty once and for all.

"If this place truly exists, I want to go there also," Kaguvi said. "I want to be with Jesus in paradise."

Father Richertz smiled at Kaguvi. He hugged him gently and whispered in his ear: "You've made the right choice for your life, my son, and it is one you'll never regret."

***

Back in the prison yard, Chiri had been standing among the crowds, looking at his sister, Charwe, walking towards the hanging tree. The air was thick with tension, and the crowd's hushed murmurs seemed to echo in his ears. The noose hung from a thick branch, swaying slightly in the breeze. He had never seen a person being hanged before, but he had heard stories from fellow inmates, the desperate gasps and the futile struggles. He couldn't imagine watching that happening to his sister, his poor Charwe. It had been long since he had seen her, and she looked miserable, walking to the tree that was meant to take her away. He could hardly recognise the woman that had crowned him as Chief. Charwe wore her same old torn and dirty dress, and she was as pale as she was thin. Her steps were slow, deliberate. Her hands were bound, and she looked calm and composed as the guards led her to the gallows.

Chiri wanted to cry because he could only see his poor sister, the one he had grown up with, the one that was always scared. He could see that she was forcing on a mask that was not fitting for her face. She wanted to look strong, but he could see the weakness and terror that she was so much trying to hide. He felt a surge of anger and fear, mixed with a desperate longing to hold her, to protect her, to tell her everything would be alright.

His heart shattered with each step she took towards her impending doom. He had never been so depressed in life before.

They were taking her away from him, just as they had taken his dear Kemu. He wasn't there for Kemu, and he wanted to be there for Charwe. He was not going to let them take her away from him.

Chiri's legs moved before his mind caught up. He pushed through the crowd, running towards her, shouting her name. "Charwe! Charwe!"

The prison guards caught him before he could even get to her.

Tears streamed down his face, his voice choking with sorrow as he pleaded with the guards to let him reach her. But their grip was unyielding.

Charwe heard Chiri and turned to him. She had not seen him until then. She had been longing to see him before going. A faint smile touched her lips. "Chiri, my brave brother!"

She felt sorry for him because he looked awful. He was in dirt and rags and was as thin as some of the branches from the tree in front of her. His wound had not yet healed properly

She turned away from him, then looked up at the rope dangling from the hanging tree, as if it was mocking her inner turmoil. The noose had been waiting for her neck, to take her away from Chiri. She felt a surge of panic, but she calmed herself, telling herself it would all end soon enough.

She felt a hand on her shoulder, pushing her forward. It was one of the prison guards. She climbed the wooden steps, feeling the roughness of the planks under her feet.

She was afraid, but she kept a stern expression. Chiri had taught her that, once. The world only sees the mask you wear, not the face underneath.

Soon, she would be united with all the others, in the land of the ancestors. They were going to kill her, but not her spirit. Her spirit was going to live on in the hearts and minds of those that had been left, and they would continue with her struggle.

There was a whole world waiting for her, a world that she could safely call home.

***

Meanwhile, in the dimly lit confines of the prison chapel, Father Richertz stood before Kaguvi, whose face looked awful with sadness and despair. For the first time after his imprisonment, Kaguvi was given a new white garment to wear. Father Richertz told him that he almost looked like an angel.

Kaguvi had sorrow on him, as if he was betraying Nehanda and his people. If paradise truly existed, he was never going to see her, or Murenga and all the others. Nehanda had refused to be baptised, thus she lacked the token to be in paradise with him. He would be in a new beautiful place with people he never knew. He would even bear a new name, Dismas, the good thief.

Father Richertz, his voice filled with compassion, began the sacred ritual of baptism.

"Kaguvi, my son, today we gather here to cleanse your soul and offer you the grace of God," Father Richertz spoke gently, his words echoing through the chapel. "Through this sacrament, we seek to bring you peace and hope, even in the face of darkness."

Kaguvi, his hands trembling, looked up at Father Richertz with eyes clouded by fear and pain. He then lowered his head so that he would be baptised. He felt a tear roll down his cheek, a tear that he could not hold back any longer.

As Father Richertz poured the holy water over Kaguvi's head, a profound silence filled the chapel. The only sound was the soft splash of the water and the faint whisper of Father Richertz's prayer.

"May the Holy Spirit guide you, Dismas, and grant you the strength to face the path that lies ahead. May you find solace in God's love and forgiveness and may His mercy shine upon you."

***

At last, Charwe reached the top of the platform, where a hooded man stood with a rope in his hand. He was ugly, scary and merciless, and she could see it all under that hood of his. She then turned around to face the people, and the hooded man adjusted the noose around her neck. He asked her if she had any last words.

From the watchers, Chiri's heart pounded in his chest, threatening to burst. He strained against the guards' hold, his voice now reduced to a hoarse whisper, pleading for mercy that was destined to fall on deaf ears.

She had not seen her children for quite a while, she remembered. It felt like it had been years.

In her heart, she prayed for their safety, and protection. She prayed that they would grow old, live happy lives and have children of their own. She felt a pain in her chest when she remembered that she was never going to see any of her grandchildren.

She tried to imagine the scene of when her children would hear of her death. Hungwa would probably go and stand on the edge of a cliff and scream his anguish out. That was what he always did whenever he got angry at something.

That is why he would always storm out of the house after an argument, to go and find a place where he would be alone, where no one would hear him.

Somewhere within the crowd, she saw Chiri. Their eyes briefly met, but she quickly turned away, for it was too heavy for her heart.

At least she knew there was one person amongst the watchers that loved and truly cared for her. Chiri reminded her that she was still loved and was special.

Charwe was weak and afraid, but she knew she had to be brave for the last time. She was not going to cry or make any apologies. She was the Mhondoro and was bred by the Hwata. She was a warrior, a queen of ages, and she was glorious. She was standing in front of her enemies, and her head was still held up high. That was brave, that was bold, and that was all she needed.

She then looked in the distance and saw a bird sitting on a tree branch near her. It was the same bird that she had seen in her dream, the bateleur eagle. It was looking straight into her eyes.

The bird then flapped its wings and flew off. She finally found her last words as she looked at the bird flying away.

"A bird can land, but it will always go back to the skies. The sun can set but it will always rise. A man can die but the spirit will always awaken," Nehanda spoke with great courage, even though her voice held quite a tremble.

She then looked at her brother, Chiri, and she clenched her fists to keep herself from shaking. She had to be strong this one last time, for him. "My bones might fall today but I will never sing any song of defeat because this is not the end. Boldly, I say no, it can never end this way. My bones shall rise again." She finished her speech and closed her eyes. A single tear escaped her hold and traced a glistening path down her cheek.

The hangman pulled the lever, the trapdoor opened, the rope snapped, and Nehanda Charwe's body fell and swung in the air.

The sudden drop sent a shiver through the crowd, a collective gasp escaping their lips. The world blurred around Chiri; and he could hear nothing but the rasp of Charwe's breathless agony.

Nehanda's body swayed gently in the breeze, suspended by the unforgiving rope. The air itself seemed to weep, heavy with the loss of a legend, a great woman who deserved better.

"Charwe," Chiri whispered, tears blurring his vision. "I'm sorry I couldn't save you, I'm sorry."

Chiri's legs gave way beneath him, collapsing to the ground in a heap of despair. His anguished cries pierced the silence, a raw expression of the pain that consumed him.

It was done. Nehanda, the great heroine, was dead.

The End

Afterword

Nehanda Charwe Nyakasikana was executed on 27 April 1898 in Salisbury, modern day Harare. Her execution was followed by the executions of Kaguvi, and Chief Chiripanyanga, while Masvi was the only one pardoned for exemplary behaviour. Unfortunately, the whereabouts of Nehanda's remains remain unknown to this day.

The first Chimurenga, or uprising, came to an end, and by 1900, the British South Africa Company (BSAC) had gained full control. Despite this, the discrimination against the native population persisted. However, the people never forgot the resistance and unity that their heroes had inspired.

After more than sixty years, the Second Chimurenga broke out, proving to be even more aggressive than the first. Lasting for another 30 years, this struggle ultimately led to the natives prevailing and achieving independence by 1980. The country retained the name of its ancient kingdom from the 1500s, Zimbabwe.

Nehanda Charwe Nyakasikana was rightfully honoured as a national heroine, forever remaining an icon of the liberation struggle. She is the ultimate feminist of Zimbabwe. Her last words continue to echo in the minds of many, as a reminder that blood was once spilled.

- MY BONES SHALL RISE AGAIN! -

Acknowledgements

I would like to acknowledge the literary advocates at Book Fantastics, who made me cross paths with my publisher and editor, Samantha Rumbidzai Vazhure. I would also like to acknowledge Samantha herself for all the back and forth emails during the publishing process. Thank you for believing in the story of Charwe.

Thank you to Memory Chirere who also edited this book.

I would like to acknowledge my parents, my family, and my friends, who have been greatly supportive throughout my writing journey.

Lastly, I would like to acknowledge all the heroes and heroines, from the past to this day, who strive to fight for the freedom and happiness of others, including themselves.

About the author

Elton Ndudzo is a twenty-one year old Zimbabwean writer, currently residing in Chitungwiza. Elton was a finalist in the inaugural Carnelian Heart Short Story competition in 2024, and his short story, 'In the fold', appears in the competition anthology: *Things You Cannot Say With Your Mouth*. Charwe is his debut novel, and it evidences his interest in African history and culture. He is also a tech-enthusiast, currently pursuing a degree in Computer Engineering at Chinhoyi University.